THE END OF THE NOVEL

A NOVELLA

THE END OF THE NOVEL

A NOVELLA

Michael Krüger

Translated from the German
by Ewald Osers

GEORGE BRAZILLER
NEW YORK

PT
2671
.R736
E513
1992

First published in the United States in 1992 by George Braziller, Inc.

Published in Great Britain in 1991 by Quartet Books Limited, a member of the Namara Group

English translation copyright © 1991 by Ewald Osers

Originally published in German

Copyright © 1990 by Residenz Verlag under the title *Das Ende des Romans*

All rights reserved

For information, write to the publisher:

George Braziller, Inc.
60 Madison Avenue
New York, NY 10010

Library of Congress Cataloging-in-Publication Data
Krüger, Michael, 1943–
[Ende des Romans. English]
The end of the novel : a novella / Michael Krüger ;
translated from the German by Ewald Osers. —
1st U.S. ed.
p. cm.
Translation of: Das Ende des Romans.
ISBN 0-8076-1275-8
I. Title.
PT2671.R736E513   1992
833'.914—dc20   91-43571   CIP

ISBN: 0-8076-1275-8

Printed in the United States of America

First U.S. edition

I do not know why I was born; nor do I know how; any more than I know what the world is or what I may be myself. And if I wish to investigate the question I soon have to abandon the attempt as my ever increasing ignorance confuses me. I do not know what my body, my senses, my soul are; indeed even that part of myself which thinks about what I write and which investigates everything, including itself, will never be able to know itself. In vain does my intellect strive to measure the infinite spaces of the universe surrounding me. I feel as though I were pinned to the minute corner of a boundless space, without knowing why I am placed at this spot rather than at any other, or why the brief term of my existence is intended for this moment of eternity rather than for all those preceding or succeeding. On every side I see nothing but infinites devouring me like an atom.

Ugo Foscolo

1

I let him die. Where I found the strength simply to turn off the air for that impatient *vis-à-vis* of many years, that never wearying tormentor and dubious companion, who was so much more loquacious and intelligent than myself and whose vitality seemed inexhaustible, I could not say. Today his time is up, that was my firm decision in the morning. Just one last sentence. But no justification, no severing of any metaphysical chain by which he might feel attached to objects, and likewise nothing ironical, nothing about the time which threatened to slip away from him and about which he had endlessly talked in our nocturnal discussions, no nostalgia, no lament, of which he seemed to be a master like no one else, no *jeu de mot*, no grand gesture, no mourning, above all not the flash of realization that might help lend an expressive mask to a faceless life, as he had often affirmed when trying, by talking, to get over the death of friends, but likewise nothing technical about the choice of the instruments which were to send him to his death, to divert attention from the weighty decision, and also nothing factual concerning our relationship, the rupture of our relationship. With that final sentence he had, simultaneously, to receive life and lose it forever. That sentence, keystone of a deliberately incomplete edifice, was not easy to find among the many sentences which exalted the man, just as if, continually metamorphosing himself, he eventually only had that final sentence on his lips, a crumbling balance sheet.

By the time the sun stood at the zenith I had jotted down and discarded more than thirty sentences, developed a confused panorama of contradictory statements, in which the peripheral kept pushing to the centre, only to be squeezed back again into casualness by succeeding sentences, so that eventually I yielded and was willing to give him a little more time: he might take poison, some mild vegetable poison which would slowly paralyse him, so slowly that, in a prone position, he would have ample time to stare at the sky which would effortlessly absorb his last thoughts. Poison? Was poison still an up-to-date means of taking one's life when we are all slowly dying of poisons of our own manufacture? Should he not simply slumber away, after a sip of water, a deep breath, an impertinent sigh, a long last look at the world? No, he should have an opportunity once more to gather up his pain under the vast sky, once more to cast an instant into the infinity which enclosed his body, his life, patiently and, in a matter-of-fact way, indifferently, before closing his eyes for ever, those eyes by which he had orientated his entire life. His neuralgias, his toothache, his hypochondriacal insomnia, the itchiness of his scalp, his entire oversensitized perceptive apparatus between urge and inhibition, which he had observed day by day like a conscientious researcher and which he, a fanatical reader and life-long student, had, as it were, shored up with literary pain in order to lend it a significance that would transgress banal perception, all these torments cultivated by repetition, the torments which hearing and seeing, smelling and tasting had caused him – these could not be terminated at a single blow, without trace. Poison was out. After this kind of life he had to die deliberately, in slow motion, even though only a few sentences were needed for his ebbing away, his fading out; perhaps only words: his favourite words, hopes, curses, heresies, which would have to stand naked on the page and would make no sense, a small angular panorama, hard on the reader's eyes. Words like stigmata.

But which? Language is a graveyard of burnt-out phrases – that is what he used to say when he swaggered in the drawing-rooms, seeking to make his listeners seem contemptible.

One day, late in the evening at the pharmacy, I had got a young girl pharmacist to explain to me the action of the more common vegetable poisons and, firmly convinced that he would resort to poison, eventually decided on one which slowly relaxed the muscles, so that he would feel the pain, that glorious return of nature to the body, on which he had so often discoursed, too often perhaps, eventually leaving him. The pharmacist, who knew me as a good customer for headache and sleeping tablets and was informed on the extent of my daily poisoning, had at first only reluctantly answered my detailed questions and had not been prepared to hand over to me any indication slips, which I had hoped to photocopy in order to be able to speak as accurately as possible on absorption, effect and counter-effect. However, after some skirmishing on global living conditons on the one hand and on cosmic ones on the other, and on the necessity for not taking one's own life too seriously in order to make cosmic survival possible, she allowed me to sit down at a table behind the counter, and this was soon overbrimming with specialized toxicological literature. My little black notebook was filled by the time the night shift was nearly over. I woke the pharmacist, who, grumpily, emerged with swollen eyes from behind her screen, a four-wing wrought-iron screen with Neapolitan-genre scenes of the eighteenth century. (The two central panels were decorated with a game and wildfowl dealer's theme: plucked partridges, fattened hens and skinned hares in brilliant colours were suspended from an open door and the butcher, a cleaver in his hand, was explaining to a woman customer – who quite startlingly resembled the pharmacist – the merits of the dead meat.) She was clearly irritated that, not having stayed awake, she had not been equal to my zeal and listened with a testy expression to my announcement that I had decided in favour of a spurge preparation. The plants of the spurge family, in particular toxicodendron, had given rise to a vast quantity of learned literature which ran through the eighteenth and nineteenth centuries like a poisonous thread. Nowadays it was no longer used, at least the files of the Göttingen Institute for Suicide Research recorded no case of spurge poisoning in all the years since its foundation. But I fancied the notion that he would resort to spurge to overcome his pain, even though the specialized literature – if indeed it troubled to consult those out-of-the-way folios – might prove to me that with such preparations the expulsion of pain, as described by me, could not be accomplished. Spurge it shall be – with this sentence I had dispatched the pharmacist back behind her plucked birds and had stepped out into the street.

I bought a morning paper and scanned the positions vacant, but apart from a curious offer of a post for moral philosophy there was nothing to capture my attention. Vacancies for unleashed thinking were in short supply, thought-blocking professorships, on the other hand, were being offered *en masse*, especially out in the country, where, in the neighbourhood of industrial enterprises, they shot up, in the newly developed discipline of 'research ethics', like mushrooms from the infested soil. Never again, the research ethicists called out to the smoking chimneys which, unmoved, continued to smoke so that the job-creation programme for moral philosophers, paid for by industry, could continue to be financed. A splendid chain, I thought, the ethical hero as the victim of research with civil-service status. Whoever is no longer in the thrall of the world will either have to adapt to that chain or else drink of spurge.

I let the bus drive on and set out on foot across the hills which separated me from the village where I had been living and working in a wooden summerhouse for the past few years. In my head I tried out the sentences which were to be the last ones to be uttered by him, by his weary body, which I visualized in a deckchair in the open, an inner monologue which was slowly to unravel, expire in scraps of sentences, fragments, words. And yet his last minutes were to be so fashioned as if he had lived all his life for just that day. At last the spot, at last the right time for the spark to ignite and the foul substance to be reduced to ash. Roused from everyday existence, surveying the horizon of time, he suddenly has darkness before his eyes: and then only a call, a question, a jubilant decline and the expunction of terror.

The cows were back in their pasture and glanced at me only briefly as I passed them with a salute, the swallows were inscribing their reckless geometry in the sky, and the lake, which from the elevation here became visible in the trough, slowly filled with a seductive sparkle. On this exalted day, which seemed to elude portrayal in a logical language, he was to die so as to restore my freedom to me.

2

Through the holes in the sun umbrella quivering patches of light fell on my manuscript which a smooth stone I had brought back from Greece prevented from blowing about the garden. Enclosed in the stone is a small landscape, as though formed by mosses, a dreaming world, an Atlantis of minute houses and strangely distorted animals which effortlessly traverse the grey-hued sky, carrying off the memories of gossamer-thin stick figures standing rigid on angular streets. Who, for heaven's sake, are we, they seem to ask, in the inanimate miracle which we are part of, what mythology do we have to apply to talk ourselves out of this rigidity? Not a trace of reality is there to be followed, without trace they are lost. A tree soundlessly brushes the sky, a wind ceaselessly files down the mountain, and the words of the dead, who are entitled to their say in this simply structured world, flutter across the scenery like inscribed banners: 'And fish came to the dwellings of men, baked themselves and served themselves on a laid table . . . and roast thrushes with rolls flew into men's gullets.'

A monk on Mount Pelion had made me a present of the stone, a sun-scorched fellow who, in an English never before heard, was trying, by the example of that stone, to explain to me the risk of the Golden Age: All round him was the fluttering of the dead like that of birds when, alarmed, they scatter in all directions. The book of history, he said, had closed over us because we were no longer fit for a chapter of our own. It is no longer prepared to tolerate us.

Before me was the final page, its centre weighed down by my pencil, its corners rebelling against it, as if protesting against my decision to make it the carrier of the final sentence. The clouds over the lake had pale-pink translucent edges, from afar came the whirring noise of a lawnmower over the hump of the little hill beyond which lay the village, on the narrow path between the property where I worked and the reed-grown lakeshore stood the day's first pair of lovers, gazing, while rocking in close embrace, so peacefully into each other's eyes that they could not possibly have any inkling of the dramatic decisions that were being made a hundred yards from them. I coughed persistently in order to dispel the image of the lovers, which interfered with my formulation of the final sentences. This unsettled the swallows, which abruptly, with unbelievable speed, started into a small gap broken out of the wooden double doors of the barn which served me as my working depository during the summer.

I had patched up the leaky spots in the roof with

roofing felt, so that the summer thunderstorms, which formed over the lake and came down heavily along its edges, could not confuse or dilute my spread-out arrangment of bits of paper. A disused tractor supplied the space with a sickly smell of lubricating oil, which mingled marvellously with the smell of warm timber. In the garden house itself there was no room for my working papers, as it was filled to capacity by a narrow table, a chair, a three-part pull-out couch of the fifties, which served me as a bed, and a rickety set of pine shelves. The shelves had to accommodate the kitchen equipment, a small collection of stones and roots, a small medicine chest which had once contained Sumatra cigars, whose aroma now mingled disagreeably with my headache tablets, and a collection of tattered paperbacks which were being prevented by Frazer's voluminous *Golden Bough* from toppling on to the hotplate to which I owed not just my white coffee. There was also a television set for a black-and-white reproduction of the ridiculous national nonsense that bore no relation to the whole or to fundamentals, and a record player of the same vintage as the pull-out couch, which could be loaded with ten records at a time, which then, one after another, noisily crashed on top of each other, but in the course of it provided an invariably surprising concert. I enumerate the inventory of that cracked idyll merely in an attempt to understand my (to this day mysterious) longing for just this spot and to justify the anything but fair devices I have resorted to in order to enjoy a right of residence in this miserable cell. Only here was I able to work, this was my assigned place for discovering the tricks of the craft of creation. I had travelled halfway round the world and had visited the most bizarre places, I had rented wooden shacks in Mexico and Canada, tin shacks in Greece and Turkey, in order to be able, in quiet and solitude, to raise up and release the progeny of my intellect, and invariably, after a few weeks, discovered that basically I had done nothing else but once more copy the old texts which I had written here, in this habitation by the lake. I had invented demons and grimaces, spooks and hobgoblins, regions not found described on maps, but ultimately these were but masks whose arrested expressive power overarched the real chaos of my hero.

I thus had every reason to return here, to the lake, as otherwise there was a danger of slipping down into repetitions, digressions, belated insertions and footnotes which would turn the tightly structured thing in my mind's eye into an 'Encyclopedia of Miscellania'. Only in this askew shell was I apparently able to think and write about my hero's pain in words which satisfied my demands. Only from here was I able to follow this man everywhere, this man who was forever annoying the world with his views, and listen, excitedly or wearily, to his information on himself, conveyed at times with self-control and at times in a stammer. I had sneaked after him in all weathers, crouched in a corner as a patient stenographer during his unsuccessful amorous adventures in Haifa and Peru, so that he could – for the benefit of my notebook

– complete his embarrassing excuses, supplied him bravely though hopelessly with arguments for his political discussions whenever in the face of his interlocutors' brutality or meanness, these threatened to fail him, had provided for him (in Ankara) a getaway car when, at the time of the Junta, he was no longer able to withdraw his neck from the noose by his own efforts, and had come to his aid when an unspecified complaint detained him in the bed of a Russian *emigrée* at Harvestehude, from whose insatiability he was only able to save himself by whispered sayings of that genius Rosanov: 'The link between sex and God is greater than the link of the intellect with God, and greater also than the link of conscience with God – which is proved by the fact that all asexuals reveal themselves as atheists.'

To this day I had been his indefatigable urger-on, his guilty conscience, his endemic complaint, his friend in need. I had shown him the road which had led him through the jungle of boredom, through the vortex of opinions. And I had snatched him from happiness whenever it attempted to paralyse him. Was I now to let him off? Was I to run the risk of his appearing at my doorstep one day, whining, a flayed loser, begging to be reattached to my pencil? No, I needed my dictatorial infamy to sever him from me once and for all, and I needed an indifferent parting, banal and without explanation. Either the reasons developed over the many hundreds of pages sufficed to authorize this decision, or else there was only the classical justification: One fine day the no longer quite so young man decides to direct his utmost attention to his pain and, in consequence, to renounce his life. Whether from love of contingency, that last surprise artiste of this world, or from anger, or from profound boredom, is for the reader to decide, and no doubt our ubiquitously flourishing suicide research is now sufficiently advanced to have a suitable concept also for my case. His suicide was not to seem 'imposed', not to look like a second-best solution. Readers, I was hoping, should not think that the hero's death came a little abruptly, that it did not seem really motivated, that the assessment of his life's background actually suggested a ripe old age, etc. Death always comes a little abruptly and at the wrong moment, only in literature is it requested to be good enough to wait until the implementation of certain formal criteria justifies its intervention. An idea, a life's plan, must be led to its conclusion, only then may it strike. With me, on the other hand, it is to be the hero who calls death one day, one fine summer's day, and he is to be ready at once with his little brown bottle of spurge extract. There are a few things to be done, a few things to be thought about, concerning the world and its machinations, a conversation is to be conducted with God and a few glances to be cast into the unfathomable archives, a few words to be said about the pains which are slowly being resolved by the spurge. But after that there should be an end. I could feel the world slipping from my grasp, pain contracting into one point and travelling through the body in search of an object. I could feel every part of the body rejecting it, until, unemployed, it faded in the pit of the stomach. Or should I speak in the third person: He could feel the world slipping out of his grasp. He lay there with a strange unconcern, as if after a bungled entrance. Or should I put at the end a series of general sentences which were only indirectly concerned with the dying man, anamorphotic sentences about human existence, which invents pain to be compelled to speak and which endeavours to kill that pain in order to be allowed to be silent again? Or was there, at the end, after all only a descending ladder of disjointed words and at the end of them:

Hatred
Love
Terrible clarity?

Next to the pile of manuscripts was the mountain of my notebooks, a fallen regiment of exercise books manufactured in China, in black plastic covers with red top edges, the heart of my monstrous opus, for which it had supplied ideas over the years. Those ideas were listed in long columns on the endpapers and, when included in the novel, were furnished with a tick. I picked up the notebooks one by one and was shocked to see how many entries still lacked a tick, because the thought that the characters of my book, weighed down as they were anyway by a crushing number of views and opinions, should also have discussed, championed and rejected the as yet unticked headings made me question the concept of totality originally envisaged by me. In the more than eight hundred closely covered pages of my handwritten manuscript only one-third, on a superficial estimate, of the planned ideas had in fact been accommodated, and I was suddenly pervaded by the terrible suspicion that the unconsidered two-thirds might be the real constituent features of the characters, whom I had always thought of as boldly conceived. The very first heading in the first notebook I opened had been impossible to fit into the book, even though it was accompanied by a mass of interesting observations: transmutation of the mode of existence. It was still written in ballpen and must therefore date back to a time when I was still in touch with some circles involved in magic, in whose seances I wished to let my hero participate in his quest for the true truth. That must have been twenty years ago, I thought, and immediately felt ashamed. At that time we were in a state of heightened receptivity for the numinous, having examined rational stocks and rejected them. From that time date the first sketches of my hero, the first tentative outlines of his portrait. He was, according to my idea then, as I now well remembered, to lose all rational justification of his existence and surrender to a mystical view of the world, which was to have taken him to the verge of the delusion of being one of the Enlightened.

The material for that complex had then been easy to come by, as many of my acquaintances seemed to know their way around the shamans of the Himalayas better than around their two-roomed flats. And I, at that time, had the special good fortune to be allowed to share my flat with a girl who had the most direct kind of access to mystical circles. Although she was my subtenant and was supposed to pay her rent in terms of domestic work – a detail as, because of her mystical involvements, she was unable to pursue any regular employment – she had in no time become the ruler of our domestic community: she decided on our vegetarian diet, she arranged the few pieces of furniture according to her taste – and that, too, was only the instrument of superior inspiration – she administered the household money and effected purchases which, for the most part, served only her needs, starting with prayer mats and ending with sacred vessels in which lamp black, curds, sandalwood, honey and melted butter were stirred and preserved. She was the custodian and the listener, she was the angel of bolts and lintels. When I returned home at lunchtime from my temporary job with the post office and tried to settle down with my books I was forbidden to do so because my negative emanation disturbed the meditation in which she, along with her girl friend, a former Trotskyite, was engaged in the next room. My bedding one day landed in the passage because the vibrations in my room were allegedly detrimental to my soul. My underwear, green army surplus, was consigned to the dustbin because, allegedly, sex could not unfold in it. My books were arranged by colour and size in order to let the most disparate subjects and stories get into conversation with one another, which resulted in Marx finding himself the neighbour of Oblomov, in Pareto having to endure within a few pages of Montale, and all kinds of other odd consequences. She had already had an astonishing career in the subculture of those years behind her when, recommended by a mutual friend who was no longer keen on her palmistry, she turned up at my place. She had run a lesbian cell in Frankfurt, organized Trotskyite art history courses in Marburg, promoted a revolutionary film group 'Vertov' in Hanover (whose director now heads a consulting agency at a castle in my neighbourhood), and gained her doctor's degree at Augsburg with a dissertation on the image of the superman in Indian philosophy – all of which activities she now looked back on with fierce mockery, finding only words of contempt for those who were still active in such fields. Through Rudolf Steiner she had come to the idea of having to set out in search of lost harmony, which she supposed to exist, of all places, in my flat. And her search was thorough. Once she found the key in the Tibetan book of the Dead, another time in an African moon ritual which arrested her menstrual flow; she ceaselessly meditated and read cards, checked the flat with a pendulum and forced me, in the middle of the night, into unsuccessful intercourse because the stars were suggesting such a union. And she would fervently interpret my dreams, even when, for lack of suitable dream material, I invented something or related something I had just read. What she liked best were dreams foretelling death because in them she could prove herself as a guide through death; erotic dreams she described as acquired learning and rejected them. I always wrote everything down, the material filled many pages in my little book. And when one day during the Christmas period – I was particularly fagged out because of the quantity of mail – she informed me that she intended to stage a major seance for uniting the forces of the masculine-heavenly and the feminine-earthly, I realized that that evening would provide a kind of initiation for my hero. At issue would be the transmutation of one's mode of existence, and the participants were to be, in addition to our ex-Trotskyite woman friend, her slave if the truth be told, who by then was also more or less living with us, an assistant professor of sociology who, with a chilly glance, invariably asked everyone: But where does the spirit reside? without ever rallying sufficiently to provide an answer, his wife Beate, head of a Zen centre and a psychotherapist, her lover, a philosopher who was shunned in philosophical circles because of his cynicism, further an actress from the municipal theatre, who had broken both her legs as Käthchen in *Käthchen von Heilbronn* and was therefore available in the evening, and the woman owner of an esoteric bookshop who had her picture, in a turban, on her own bills, which I had to settle, under threat, every month. I was to supply crackers, Twiglets and lime-flower tea, as well as beer for the philosopher and hard liquor. We sat around the table in the living room, the books and pictures were shrouded, the lamp was dimmed, and we were conversationally approaching the centre-point of the evening, that authority said to be mightier than our ego. The esoteric bookseller occasionally grabbed my hand and squeezed it flabbily and heartlessly, while her fine upper body swayed like a pendulum and a hum issued from her wide mouth, intensifying in the course of the evening to a melodic moan, a drawn-out note that seemed to herald misfortune or just the unknown. Now and again there was some reading aloud, for instance on the light from the Inexhaustible Light, but it was done, I thought, very badly, the sociologist in particular being unable to utter three sentences without fluffing, which resulted in embarrassing misunderstandings about the various 'trans' states: transubstantiation and transmutation, not to mention transgredencies and translocations, among which he got hopelessly entangled. The only visible transmutation was to be observed in the cynic, who had gulped down his Obstler in record time and was displaying features of intoxication which might, to the uninitiated, suggest ecstasy. When the light was turned up again there was nothing much to be perceived except transudation. The university gentlemen seemed stiff and suffering as if after a funeral, the bookseller smiled crookedly and gently, and the actress was immediately concerned once more with her plastered legs, the left one of which she laid in the lap of the drunken philosopher who actually, with stupid expression, brandished a fountain pen, endeavouring to score a point against his opponent with the scribbled sentence: 'The spirit lives here!'

I had, at some point or other, locked myself in the

lavatory and, under the heading 'Transmutation of mode of existence', written seven pages and furnished them with notes on how I hoped to fit them into my book: My hero was to set off for the jungle with a group of like-minded persons, so they could jointly intoxicate themselves with all kinds of exotic practices in the hope of overcoming the mediocrity they were suffering from and which they saw as the result of Western civilizatory developments. Exactly how I had pictured that transmutation was no longer to be gathered from the notes, except that my mind-burdened hero disappeared into the jungle with a local shaman and only reappeared among his group weeks later, a different person. Man is a masterpiece of failure, I had jotted down; with these words he was to hail his former companions. He was then to have been disgusted by the hybrid manner in which these diagnosed their lives' problems and to have decided to return to civilization on his own to surrender passively to the terror of everyday dreariness, to surrender discouraged to the terror of politics: no more struggle, no more display of courage, thus ran my final note under that heading, which, however, was no longer used in the writing down of the final version of my novel because the hero, in the course of the sloughings of his skin, in contrast to the first concept, was fighting ceaselessly against life and history and was to summon up all the courage he was capable of in order not to find himself, a ridiculous figure, on the losing side. His many journeys – I later decided – were not to lead him beyond Europe and, as a rule, to serve commercial purposes and not enlightenment. On the contrary, this Hermes as a rule returns defeated and is then given an opportunity to analyse his defeat, moreover with an eloquence which contrasts strangely with the helplessness of his reaction to the blows he suffers. Should I, in retrospect, add another chapter on yang and yin in order to accommodate at least a part of the surplus material on the sociology of the saint, which filled two more copybooks and was subdivided from 'Rebirth in the Indian light' to 'Questions of Tantra-Yoga'? Better not. Instead I should, and would, apply my whole strength to the final sentences, which would probably decide how my work of so many years was assessed. If the composition of these sentences were not to be successful I might as well destroy the whole manuscript. I was therefore compelled to concentrate all the remnants of energy still dormant in me after the reworking of the manuscript, now due, to fan that crucial fire whose flickering glow would place the over-long structure in the right light – or else I must not let the hero die but must write on to the end. Either that final sentence – this was the alternative before my eyes as I looked down towards the lake which was now slowly taking on a leaden hue – or death.

I had suspicion of what I would be faced with during the next few months. The reworking and copying of the manuscript would have to be completed by the end of the year; until then it might be possible to stretch my debts. Until November I could stay in the garden house, after that a warm room would have to be found. I fetched the laundry basket and stowed away the manuscript and the notebooks, put it in the woodshed and carefully locked the door. Later I would go over the hill to the village inn and have something to eat. The hero's death had to be celebrated.

3

At the gate which led from the property towards the lake one of the two women from next door was waiting for me: a short sturdy person in bib-and-brace trousers of indescribable colour, precariously held up by two slipping braces. She had run out of food, mineral water and cigarettes. Once a week one of the two would come to borrow something, the next day the other would call to return the loan. Perfect surveillance. Both were equally nosy, importunate and suggestive, both were predominantly engaged in defamation and had a downright scientific approach to gossip. Both of them, under varying spotlights, played leading roles in my book, indeed certain of their qualities and expressions had lent colour and outline to all the women in my book. The one now facing me had been married to a writer who, in the thirties and forties, had written a number of superficial novels which brought him world-wide fame and wealth. Because he was homosexually inclined he never stayed with any woman for any length of time, his affairs and escapades were as famous as his writings. Four times in succession he had married his secretaries, all of whom had evidently been fired by the hope of pulling him over to the other shore, as his last wife put it, but in vain. *On the Other Shore* was the title of one of his books, which had always been misinterpreted as a political allegory. When he suffered a stroke he was still married to the woman now facing me, but had already started a new affair with his new secretary, who had relieved the wife (who on marriage had to discontinue her desk work), moreover an affair which, as I often had to listen to, held good hope of finally diverting the man from his unnatural propensities. His wife and his secretary, it was stated in his will, were to look after his literary estate, they were both to continue living in the house where he had committed his nonsense to paper, they were both, in a sisterly manner, to share his estate and never remarry. You have both of you possessed the same man, he is reported to have said as he breathed his last, now go on living for his greater glory.

They had started by dismissing the gardener, whom the master had possessed much more often than he had either of them, then they changed their bank, because the branch manager, a decent chap who also handles my account, had come up once a week for intercourse, and eventually even the postman, a father of four boys, was transferred because he had boasted at the inn of having delivered more than just his letters. It had not been easy for the village to recover from these scandals, but for me they were a goldmine. The reports alone in our local paper, which I was able to adopt almost verbatim, accounted for a good twenty pages of my manuscript because they supplied splendid illustrations for an account of the moral situation of the sixties. The writer served my hero as a kind of father, who unselfishly introduced him to the art of writing: The novel is the monumental companion piece of life, that was his instruction which made my hero stumble into his hopeless endeavour of creating an overall portrait of life.

After the master's death the two women were then alone together, engaged in preparing a historical-critical edition of the deceased's works and correspondence – quite an enterprise since the author's inglorious past, which was, step by step, emerging into the light of day, always had to be interpreted, for and by the younger generation, as an act of protest. Frequently changing but invariably young German scholars therefore inhabited two attic rooms in the house, from the small windows of which they could sometimes be seen gazing hollow-eyed at the lake, because in addition to their editorial work – the texts were to be based on the manuscripts because the printed books had allegedly been disfigured through censorship beyond recognition – which was a cleaning up of thoroughly messy texts, their duties – in return for free bed and board – also included assisting the two women, who for their part exacted from the young university men all that which the writer had refused to give them. One of the young gentlemen, who once confided in me and therefore found himself included in my manuscript, had written a brilliant doctoral thesis on the doctrine of the sublime and the theory of the conduct of life in Protestant Christianity in the age of Enlightenment and was now compelled not only to expunge the regular Heil Hitler under the author's letters but also to service his last secretary, which induced the writer's widow to claim double that performance for herself. The woman in her shot-coloured bib-and-braces did not look as if she was responsible for the emaciation of German studies – a discipline suffering from emaciation and shrinkage anyway – and had she not herself shamelessly reported her escapades in every detail one might have regarded her as an utterly unliterary Hausfrau. But no sooner had I meekly handed her my last bottle of mineral water, three cigarettes and a chunk of bread, than she described to me, with feigned outrage, how the German scholar at present working at her place – from Göttingen! – a shrivelled little man with a *summa-cum-laude* thesis on the concept of melancholy in the German lyrical poets of the late middle ages compared with the crisis of enthusiastic artistry in the early Romantic age, how that little squirt – a word I determined to remember – had approached her with bloodshot eyes and panting breath, had grabbed her to him and in that grabbing more or less undressed her. And already she was demonstrating to me how easy it was to undress a woman in bib-and-braces, just look, she suddenly called out, that's how I stood there, his hands – and she took my hands – on my breasts – and placed them on her breasts – and because I thought the man was going insane, since all German scholars are potential insanity cases, lunatics diving into footnotes to conceal their insanity, I pretended to yield to him, just as the master described it in the final chapter of *On the Other Shore*. But it didn't come to the extreme, premature ejaculation, as so often observed among Göttingen German scholars, mortification, a dreadful sight, apologies. And such a person expects to become a civil servant for life, she said, and let my sopping-wet hands drop from her breasts, picked up what she had come for and walked away. Tomorrow the other will come, I thought to myself as I watched her leave, the secretary, and she would complain about German scholars from Konstanz, who constructed theories from dry-as-dust perception and not from necessity, a pile of waste paper. Distasteful, I thought, repulsive. Literature should not have an author, on no account should widows and lovers have the right to disposal over literary estates, not even the estates of third-rate authors. I returned to the woodshed, fished out my manuscript and removed all the passages, in so far as I could find them, which had anything to do with the writer as the spiritual father of my hero, and tore them up into tiny pieces. I had to sacrifice some forty pages in order to expunge all memories of my neighbour. The manuscript mountain now looked smaller, clearly shrunk, cored: but it had had to be done, the trimming was necessary to allow the shape of the whole to emerge more clearly.

4

Back at work I intended also to correct the link-ups so as not to expose my hero to any ruptures. But the disagreeable task of rewriting the biography of a relative stranger, who had grown out of oneself without one's having been able to control that growth by experience, this task now, after his death, seemed to me even more contemptible than before. The words refused to comply, they encapsulated themselves, they withdrew, they displayed no interest in me or my manuscript. The rhythmical law by which I intended to structure them seemed like some clapped-out knocking, all pliancy was gone. But this insubordination was not all. For now, during retouching, my hero also showed some signs of how used, devalued and stale he had become over the period of his creation, of my writing. The corrosive solitude which he loved so much as a contrast now revealed itself as a helpless narrator's mask, his social receptiveness, which I had so carefully contrived in order to differentiate him from other literary characters, was no longer capable of outweighing his ironical proclivity towards maliciousness, the words of salvation and benediction, which at other times offset his lack of indiscretion, turned into cold rootless cordiality. A good hour later I had sacrificed another thirty pages in an effort to spare my doomed hero at least a total reversal of his existence. Ten per cent of the manuscript had gone in a trice.

At this moment of loss I felt an urgent need to make a number of further cuts for reasons of clarity. The man knew too much. Even for a novel of development, which after all could take a good deal of substance, the book was overloaded with knowledge. I wanted to represent the hero more simply, furnish him with greater curiosity, and at the same time cut down on the discourses in which he was able to give full rein to his inexhaustibility. A person who knows everything becomes uninteresting to the reader; a person who knows everything, my hero informed me, becomes indifferent towards phenomena. A person who can explain everything is regarded as a know-all: and nothing is more dangerous or morally more reprehensible than a know-all. But the intention was easier than its realization: the longer I reflected on why the indiscretion of knowledge had captured such a dominant space in my manuscript, the harder it was for me to make sensible cuts, so that, in order to come to an end at all, I removed entire passages which, collectively, amounted to some eighty manuscript pages, the work of nearly a year, as I realized gloomily as the scraps of paper were dropping into the dustbin like cheerful snowflakes. Because on no account did I wish to preserve eliminated sections in order to publish them as independent stories, a practice I had always regarded as despicable in other authors. How much does a person have to say? This was going to be a novel, my novel, if possible the ultimate novel.

5

Nine years of writing, not counting the preparatory work – that's what I had devoted to my book, each day I had formulated my sentences, tempered in affection or in hate, and added them to the manuscript either directly or by way of the black notebooks, for nine years I had shaped that mountain range of words, that landscape with singing trees, with sun, moon and seasons, with intersecting paths and mutually repelling glances, the landscape which my hero, that avid contemporary, the insatiable, would hasten through on his restless quest, for eight hundred pages tormented by the question of whether he was on the right road to mastery over sense, mastery over the senses, or whether he had already lost his way in the maze of the contemporary, in the offside and in the dark, where life can no longer strike root and the constellations are better guides than man, whence a return, a new start, would be impossible. I had allowed him to sweep up anything in his path, men, ideas, political programmes and aesthetic manifestos,

I had recorded his defeats and his triumphant sense of happiness, his passion for anything new, which he devoured, digested and again excreted to make room for something even newer, I had channelled the flow of words that poured out over the pages and, when it threatened to dry up, enriched it with new material. The new, that noblest and most poisonous nourishment which the century had conjured upon the rickety table of time, to which all had hastily helped themselves to the point of vomiting, and were continuing to help themselves, this my hero had allowed to melt on his tongue and had swallowed in crude mouthfuls, the new woman and the new aesthetic, the new quality of politics and the new painting, the new awareness of one's body and the new media, that whole bric-à-brac of the new he had accepted, licked, torn up and chewed up, and at the end of that Pantagruelesque absorption of nutriment, the hero, aged about forty and not really despairing, serenely talking about his sufferings rather than being dominated by the will to overcome them, had made a full stop. With gloomy consistency he had recognized his indefatigable thirst for life as a projection of his loneliness, and he was no longer to be allowed to transform this realization into fresh energy in the melting pot of his curiosity. No more talk. Not another word. Nothing new. Finish.

I could see that I had to get used to the idea of his demise. Anyone who has over nine years – aside from insignificant encounters – known only a single main character, who had become the all-dominant demon of his life, a mirror reflecting more than one oneself was prepared to display, must suffer not only from withdrawal syptoms and deprivation anxieties, from ruinous compulsive ideas which corrode the remains of his being; he already finds himself at an observation post with full-time regular instruction. Others have a family, an occupation, they meet with friends at a regular table or at literary events or in bowling alleys, and generally have so arranged their lives that beneficial relations exist between body and soul; I, by contrast, had only him, a person on paper, whose eccentricity and exaltation I loved and who, at the same time, suited my intellect. All that was over now.

I was reminded of the time when I had reached about page 500. Even then I wanted to discontinue, to put an end to it. All the powers of seduction that I was able to summon within me were not enough to make me take up my pencil again, all the delight I normally derived from writing had yielded to paralysing boredom. Instead of working I would swim out in the lake, roam irritably through the forest or sit at the inn. There I one day met a woman who may boast of having driven me back to my desk. The cynical complacency with which she would discourse on works of art in order, in the shadow of such remarks, to sing the praises of life, of naked life, so incensed me that I could not help deciding once more in favour of my solitary work. The woman was undergoing live-cell treatment in the nearby village. Her husband was a spectacle manufacturer with sado-masochist inclinations, as she put it, who was glad to get her out of the house from time to time because his unusual sexual practises called for more spacious settings, which were in danger, through the presence of a more or less non-participant, of losing some of their brilliance. What it was all about was nothing less than momentary, temporary strangulation by means of a rope, from which her husband expected an erection with ejaculation, though he rarely achieved it because the artificially induced suffocation process involved the risk of a premature cardiac arrest, which, as often as not, made him call off the exercise just before achieving an erection. In consequence, strangulation had to be repeated several times, which imprinted a mask-like facial expression on the man, which, as the wife put it, made a live-cell treatment on her part an unpostponable necessity: she simply could not bear to look at him any longer. A church becoming a sheep-pen. The woman was interested in the arts, and one of the results of her husband's shame at his proclivity was a quite respectable collection of pictures which she had, item by item after each aborted strangulation, hung on her walls. Thus each of them pursued their hobbies, accusing the other of spending too much money, although both of them realized that the husband, if only for reasons of prudent precaution, had to dispense far greater amounts on a discreet domestic staff than any artist could ever expect to receive for his drawings. Ordinary mortals like us can slip behind a bush, and after ten minutes everything is over that nature demands of us, she exclaimed to me across the beef olives which at our inn are served with gherkins, in the way grandmother used to, whereas Hans needs not only three women assistants in special attire but also several medical instruments, not to mention the hush money which bears no relation to the desired effect, if indeed in Hans's case one may speak of effect at all. Thus she merrily continued with her conversation, informing me in the most irresponsible manner about the most debased matters, without pangs of conscience or shame setting out before me and explaining certain practices which to her evidently did not seem to contain anything blameworthy, so that I felt completely entitled to assume that she lacked all delicacy in moral respects.

Thus it was no more than logical that, when we had finished our meal, she requested that she might see my house and the manuscript I had been telling her about in response to her questions, a request that was more like a demand and could scarcely be declined as I had nothing but pettymindedness to set against the pleasure of her wish. We therefore walked arm in arm through the dark to my cell, and before we had even got to the woodshed she drew me to her breast, forced me to the ground and satisfied herself, not without ceaselessly explaining that only in this way was a return to paradise possible. I certainly did not share her view, but I was unable, in the under-position forced upon me, to protest – a position, moreover, which would not have done my writing-strained back any good even if I had followed the actions performed on me with any pleasure. After completion she dragged me to the lake, where we had to wash one another, then she ordered me into the house, where she immediately settled on the couch and asked me to read my manuscript to her. Read the final chapter, she commanded, that should do for a first impression. Now that final section then was a longish discourse on sin: that is, the question was discussed of whether sinful behaviour still existed in our society, a delicate question which I had accommodated in a dialogue between my hero and a woman practising prostitution, a key chapter, incidentally, for the portrayal of my hero's moral-ethical make-up. While I was thus reading my prose, pacing out hell and tracking down evil in all the corners in which it was lurking, while I was following the trail of that restless soul as it hastened round ever wider circles of the deviant, my strange woman friend fell asleep. A piping snoring struck my ears as I reached the to me important passage where I commended man's misery as his real greatness, so that I was forced to break off in the middle of the sentence in order to consider the effect of my ideas on humanism in its extreme shape. At the time, I now remembered very clearly, I wanted to attribute the concupiscent woman's sleep only to the exhausting effect of her live-cell treatment, but now I was suddenly seized by the fear that her rapid dropping-off might have had something to do with my excursions into the sphere of desecration. I therefore began to search the pile of paper for the chapter in question, which eventually I found and once more read through carefully. It disgusted me. With horror I read the discursive passage on misery and nakedness, on the ethics of sin which I had developed with grandiloquence and which came to the conclusion that only he who is capable of acknowledging the laws of sin has a chance of becoming like himself. With distaste I read aloud to myself the answers of the prostitute, who, with naïve shrewdness, arrived at the conclusion that she alone could be a true human being, if she had correctly understood my hero's expositions. Only the outsider, I read, is identical with himself because he alone knows how unique he is in this non-identical world. The self-assurance with which that whore confused my hero and prevented him from rousing his vision of hell into real life so outraged me that I decided on the spot to destroy the entire chapter. Forty pages I withdrew from the manuscript, with relief, and tore them up into ever smaller snippets until my need for extinction was satisfied.

This further spontaneous shortening of my work so intoxicated me with joy that it even checked the resurgent memory of the night with the sleeping woman: for no sooner had I then ceased my reading of the chapter on sin that the woman had woken up again and commanded me to lie down with her and perform actions which in sinfulness towered high above those mentioned in the manuscript. I had honestly tried to comply with her instructions, even though they nipped in the bud any libido that was about to arise, and at some point or other I had been compelled to break off the performance because the body postures which I was being encouraged to adopt made me fear permanent damge to my already twisted back. Nonsense, I had exclaimed, arrant nonsense, return my genital to me at once, which was then in fact, with a moist plop, released from its distressing position, though to this day I have no clear idea from what kind of anchorage its release had been accomplished. The woman left, I went on writing, and, as if intoxicated, wrote the ensuing forty-two chapters of the book, which could now easily dispense with the missing pages. And with serene satisfaction after that permitted vandalism I at last set out for the village.

6

A deep red sun was setting over the western shore; in the south, over the tip of the lake, it looked like a thunderstorm which, if it broke, would certainly reach my shore too. I was already beginning to feel a wind as I climbed the slope behind the house and trotted across the meadow in which young cows were practising crazy caprioles, halting abruptly, goggling, viewing the late visitor with heads held at an angle. One heifer, with its reeling gait and a weak eyelid muscle (of the right eye) resembled a reputed philosopher I had met at Lindos many years ago. I was forced to laugh as I suddenly recalled the episode which had lain for a long time in a dusty corner of my memory, without so much as uttering a peep, not even at the time when I was working on the cognition-theory chapters of my book, which could certainly have done with some light relief. I shall probably have to write it anew from the start, I said out loud, and then my namesake can have a small part to play, be allowed to provide a cue in the extensively covered panel discussion on the question: 'Do we need a new ethics?', which stood at the centre of the chapter and concluded with the dubious programme of a planetary macro-ethics which was to characterize the transition from conventional to post-conventional morality, a programme, incidentally, which was to reflect mankind's adolescence crisis, which quite simply did not develop the way the philosophers had expected. No one, my hero said in the above-mentioned panel discussion, keeps to established norms unless they yield him an advantage, not even philosophers, certainly not those who are fond of talking more than is good for them or their ideas. After that the representatives of historicism and hermeneuticism are given the floor again.

The philosopher of Lindos, of whom I was reminded by the sight of the friendly cow, answered to the same first name as myself, we both made use of the Socrates Café as our study, and always leapt up together when the landlord bellowed our name across the premises because one of us was wanted on the telephone. It was always he who was allowed to take it, I never received any calls, nor indeed any letters. Instead I was able to watch, almost daily, as the philosopher returned to his table confident of victory, flung down a few coins beside his cup, picked up his papers and disappeared. Once I was at the café ahead of him when our name was called. It was Ina, who acted as caretaker at the house of a German producer in the neighbouring village and was evidently feeling a need for philosophical instruction. I had overheard many a conversation between her and the philosopher from the next table, and taken them down in writing because they were interesting from the lexical point of view: some of the words have gone, as scintillating gems, into the chapter on pornography and violence in my novel. Ina took my monosyllabic early-morning voice for that of the philosopher and invited me to breakfast, but she whispered this, in itself innocent, invitation into the mouthpiece in such a strangely hushed manner that the most beautiful utopias began to luxuriate in my fantasy, readily arousable as it had become from prolonged solitude. As I was leaving the café in order to make my way through the lazy indolence of the landscape, the philosopher walked in, so that for a few seconds we faced each other eye to eye. Worked right through the night, he grunted, Fichte, always Fichte, and in this heat. On this island Fichte would never have become what he became in Berlin, he opined, which cast a gloomy light on the expected publication of my namesake. Any calls, he asked, but I had by then dived into the blinding light of the morning.

Ina was surprised to have to welcome a non-philosopher, but not disinclined to receive me because she was in urgent need of help with the watering of her plants, which, limp and dusty, were drooping under the sun. Ina was a biologist and was engaged in a diploma thesis on the Linnean system, which she intended definitively to refute and to unhinge. I nodded my head worriedly, but kept stubbornly silent so as not to impede her flow of words which I was firmly determined to memorize for my chapter on the aimlessness of scientific speech. German universities evidently still went in for refutation, moreover for the systematic refutation of systems over whose soundness generations of other researchers had spent a lifetime. The extent to which Ina in particular might feel qualified to unhinge Linneus was revealed by the fact that, during our joint watering of the garden, she was unable to identify even a single plant, indeed she was not even able to approach an identification. Barebosomed she stood by my side, her spectacles on her bony nose, despairingly holding a faded leaf of common knotgrass between her fingers – but not one word issued from her lips. What on earth can that be, I finally heard her say, never seen it before, and already she was tucking leaf after leaf into her tanga, for later identification. Breakfast consisted of a cup of coffee and a tomato, of gazing at the leaves which lazily drooped over the edge of the sunbathing garment, and of a meaningless conversation on self-relativization in complex systems, which was conducted, rather one-sidedly, by myself. But the tomato was delicious, and the presence of the almost naked biologist did not greatly impair its flavour. Quite casually I touched upon the topical aspects of Fichte's theory of science, in order on the one hand to test the theoretical capacity of my *vis-à-vis* and on the other the influence of the philosopher, whose preparatory work, however, proved of slight value. For suddenly the sun-tanned woman mumbled that in this climate Fichte would certainly never have become the person he became in Königsberg, certainly not a professor with tenure or at best B2. And with that statement she settled on a sun-lounger, undid the loop of her tanga and peeled all the limp leaves off her stomach; these could be detached only partially and only with my active assitance. Because conversation between a person sitting and a person prone, between a sitting sceptic and a prone refuter, under full solar irradiation could not attain any serious theoretical depth, I lay down beside Ina on the lounger and at some point or other fell asleep. I woke up through the hand of the philosopher, who was lightly fondling my shoulder, and cautiously rolled off so as not to wake the sleeper, and along with the Fichte scholar disappeared into the cool kitchen, where we enjoyed the German producer's very drinkable wines right through to the afternoon. Thus began our fleeting friendship, which we maintained, with never flagging indifference, throughout the summer. He later became professor of philosophy at some paedagogical college in the southwest, and although he never published a book he could, now and again, be seen on television, where he would be questioned on ethical problems of unemployment and where he adopted a stance on abortion issues. Our meagre correspondence – for the most part holiday greetings – petered out after his dismissal from office had become necessary because he had only authorized the award of degrees on grounds of achievement if these were also paid for by the assignment of apartments. As a property owner and philosopher he then increasingly devoted himself to politics and eventually finished up as Secretary of State for Education somewhere in the south-east. But I am grateful to him not for his utterly unsuccessful aberrations on culture and morality, but for the fact that, in his gloomily frivolous manner, he had opened my eyes to the strivings of philosophers, none of whom, in his opinion, had any cognitional objective any longer: the philosophers are the companion piece of philosophy in the most melancholical meaning of the word, this was one of his concluding sentences at the Socrates, when women called him away by telephone.

Under the impact of my conversation with that scholar in the kitchen of the German producer, in the immediate proximity of the biologist roasting in the sun, I subsequently sketched out a scene of the novel, where a philosopher, after the conclusion of a philosophical congress, proclaims the end of his discipline. Not, however, in plenary session, where sufficient mention had anyway been made of vanished and fragmentized man in emotional or cynical obituaries, as though no one were certain whether his departure should be jubilantly welcomed or had long been foreseen, therefore not in the conversational language peculiar to most philosophers, which has little in common with philosophy, but after the congress, at the festive final dinner, at which the philosophers' wives were also allowed to be present and where, in the main, questions of philosophical careers, salary problems and holiday venues which might be combined with future philosophical congresses added spice to the conversation. At that suitable opportunity the philosopher in my novel, a schoolfriend of my hero's, was to give the so-called ladies' address, in which, to the great dismay of the guild, he proclaimed the end of philosophy on the one hand and the end of his own university career on the other, without, however, as actually expected, uttering a single word about the ladies. I had drafted a very pretty scenario for the activities following his address: the linguistic philosophers with cynical grins assembling at the champagne bar and triumphantly toasting each other because they had always predicted that end, the last Hegelians, on the other hand, crowding around the speaker, trying to make him revoke his views in order to prevent the profession from falling entirely into the power sphere of the modern apocalyptics, many of whom had arrived in their Porsches much to the annoyance of the Hegelians who favoured Volkswagen Passats and Opels, and an utterly drunk French philosopher of Latin American extraction, whom everybody had taken for a waiter, finally grabbing the microphone and several times shouting into the hall: The end of philosophy is its beginning!', whereupon the Hegelians decide to adopt that exclamation as the motto for the next philosophical congress.

All that came back to me as I stood in the meadow in the last gloaming, regarding the friendly cow with the drooping right eyelid. And I decided to scrap from my manuscript all that longing for liberation and salvation which, despite everything, I associated with

Western philosophy. I therefore returned to the house, fetched my work, and under the lamp, with a sense of relief, removed large chunks of the eleventh and the whole of the twelfth chapter, nearly thirty pages, which, not without some inner excitement, I burnt in an old gherkin barrel.

7

It was nearly dark when once again I faced the cows which were still calmly tugging at the grasses. Frequently the animals would come down the slope as far as my fence and push their shaggy heads through the barbed wire because, for some reason or other, they particularly liked the grass in my garden, and sometimes I would have to get up and pull up the weeds for them and chuck them over to them because I could not bear the sight of the extended heads between the barbed wires. Come on, this too is only fodder, I would call out to them as at first they retreated and then, overwhelmed by my offer, accepted the blades with delicate snorts. Because these friendly animals were often in fact my only contacts, I sometimes quite seriously hoped to hear a mooed 'Thank you', even though I felt ashamed of such expectations – because if things were properly ordered in this world I should have felt ashamed of any gratitude on their part. In the end therefore I was quite proud if, through the barbed wire, they licked my hands, which, happy with this rough benefaction, I could interpret to my heart's delight. If we hadn't all been messed up by Darwin and his successors, I often thought in such situations, we would have to rewrite natural history. Even though everything is too late and natural history can only be written now as a mediocre novel, with illustrations from old Buffon or Brehm. The present is no longer recognizable under the microscope.

Of course the cows occurred in my manuscript in various chapters, and as I was now watching them in the flesh, and they me, the thought struck me that in the printed version I might unite all the cow passages into a triumphal monument, into an apotheosis of the cow, if not indeed of all horned animals with their indescribably beautiful ruminative muzzles. Perhaps, it occurred to me, the more casual mentions of cows, especially in the final two chapters, would not combine into an overall view of cows, such as I was then envisaging, and on no account should the reader of my work get the idea that the cow only played a subordinate role in my hero's picture of the world. If I remember correctly, the first cow appeared in a chapter in which the hero and a friend have a meal at a garden restaurant while the woman whom they both claim to love has gone off to a telephone box about a kilometre away. No doubt, they suspect, she will call a third friend, whom neither of them knows, which lends a practical dimension to their initially theoretical discussion which began with the ineradicability of the concept of the small family and almost casually captured the slippery slope of jealousy. As the woman sets out for the telephone she has, as if in slow motion, to walk very slowly behind a herd of cows which occupies the whole width of the road and is probably being driven into the cowshed for milking. The woman friend then is gone for so long, for all of twenty closely covered pages, that eventually she has to walk back once more behind the meanwhile milked cows which are then on their way back to their pasture, moreover so slowly that the two friends have ample time to analyse in great detail the changes in her features beyond the swaying cows, which leads to a violent quarrel and ends in the immediate departure of the friend and the rising hopes of the hero. A physiognomist and an addict of psychology are here crossing swords, two philosophies clash, an old friendship breaks up – this, roughly, would describe the situation as I portrayed it. But this was not all. In order to lend this (anyway tense) scene additional dynamism the hero, after the eventual return of the woman friend, appropriates the arguments of his now absent friend in order to present his views on jealousy, believing that his own arguments would not be shared by the woman, but is made to discover that his loved one, for her part, upholds the view, originally championed by the hero against his friend, of jealousy as the ultimate reflection of passion (*vis-à-vis* herself and others). Becuse the hero is too proud to admit to his change of sides, switched through fear, he now has to accept the departure also of his loved one, who takes her leave with a lengthy monologue and hurries after the other friend who – this was not spelled out but left to the reader's imagination – was now in for a rude awakening. The chapter concluded with a longish discourse on mask selection and trial speech, on the younger generation's inability to accept, even experimentally, another person's arguments in order to get to the root of a problem, and because I had then felt that I had filled the chapter with too much theory I let it conclude with a passage that was to hold out some pleasure for the hero. He is therefore sitting at his table, abandoned, and, as in conventional novels, is coming intellectually to terms with the defeat he has suffered, when a beautiful woman joins him at his table on the grounds that someone so busily writing could not be any threat to her. Where a moment before the adored but now vanished loved one had sat there was now, as he looked up, a magnificent chaste woman, an unhoped-for exchange which sends the hero into a state of euphoria and makes him embark on a rhetorical master performance which melts the chaste woman's heart. They spend the night and three further chapters together, until one day he discloses to her the story of the switch, whereupon she – trembling with jealousy – gets up and disappears for ever into another life.

This whole action, in its heart-rending mundane character, I had myself once experienced, moreover at the very inn that I was now making for. It had had an unpleasant sequel. One day I received from just that woman, who had meanwhile married the programme director of a private television station – an ugly, untalented power-seeker who, after every scandal that he was responsible for, had been further promoted and who, as artistic director, was about to level down the entire public television system to his own stupidity – a letter to the effect that she would take me to court if I were to publicize our fleeting contact, as she put it, and which I well remembered as one of violent desire, in the form of a book. At least she, who in truth was anything but chaste and beautiful, had respect for and a fear of literature, a long-since unusual attitude in a society dominated by indifference.

This story, one of the genuinely comic ones in my manuscript, was to serve me as a palpable illustration of a certain communication model which had time and again caught my attention, not only in politics, which seemed to follow that scheme on principle, but now, face to face with the goggling cows, I no longer felt quite so sure that the reader would recognize the fundamental model behind the drastic comedy of the scenes portrayed. I would either have to sacrifice that chapter also or else pull together and sharpen three chapters, which meant that in the first case I would lose about forty pages and in the second up to fifty. In spite of the descending darkness I sat down in the meadow and, with insects swarming about me, made some preliminary notes, also in order to outline the good idea of linking the cow passages into a definite cow chapter. One insect in particularly, which I had been unable to find even in Fabre, had long been captivating my interest: a point-sized black creature which, as it were, fell from the sky, stung without warning, and was off again without any perceptible flying motions. I also made some notes on that because these creatures, with their penchant for sudden attack, which apparently came from nowhere and vanished to be never seen again, might very well, at a certain point in the manuscript, illustrate a theory of my hero which, in recollection, had always seemed too colourless to me.

From the top of the hill the village could be seen: some twenty houses, as if huddled together for warmth, crowding round the market place, framed by farmsteads. Dairying is the rule here everywhere, with a little tourism, holidays on a farm, so the children could see a chicken before, plucked, it appeared on their plates. Not a horse far and wide, not a pig, not a goose, only cows and chickens. No grain, no potatoes or beet, only grass and clover and wild flowers luxuriating on the rich soil. A footpath led along the crest of the hill, furnished with seats provided either by the municipality or by specifically named donors. I sat down and looked at the darkening lake, on which white horses had now appeared, an infallible sign of an approaching thunderstorm. The tall trees on the bank crowded into the water so that the boundary dividing the lake from the shore was no longer discernible.

How often had I sat here and made notes about the lake. Even the material I had used for the great sea voyage from Italy to Greece and Turkey, during which the hero discovers himself, was whenever water is mentioned – and water is mentioned continually –

observed from this lake, which now began to seethe before my eyes. The wind was whipping the little tree by my seat and piling up the waves below, the cows began to low anxiously while a few courageous birds whirred past me twittering noisily. The strange scenery, which, even though it belonged to this lake and was entirely familiar to me, filled me with a sense of happiness that bore no comparison to anything else. Besieged by thunderstorms was the title of a chapter in my book, which now, as I was once more besieged by these thunderstorms as though by wild animals, seemed to me inadequate as an attempt to place a man's inner disposition in relation to the weather. On the other hand, my life (and my hero's life), which I spent out here, drew its strongest impulses from nature and not from people, who occasionally glided across my horizon, dimming it, and a thunderstorm was more apt than conversation to render transparent the thin boundary between internal and external world. Lightning now struck like an axe-blow, runnels of water rushed hissing through the grass, the path down the slope suddenly resembled a brown bubbling stream over which I had to leap several times in order to reach the inn with reasonably dry feet. And yet this leaping, this flailing of arms was a far stronger reviving element for my thoughts than the vision of shortly sitting at the bar.

I was soaked to the skin and shivering when the houses suddenly stood before me, veiled in wisps of mist and rain, surrounded by a strange brightness that seemed to come not from the lit windows but as if the last rays of the sun were being reflected. I had often observed such phenomena in our region, and even made use of them as far as I was able to describe them. In my description of nature I had tried to convey the impression pure, without comparison, as it were without gloss, to leave it its unfathomable dignity, but whenever I remembered details of my account, of how I had tried, a hundred times, to put the rain down on paper, to describe the noise, the light over the suddenly darkening fields, I despaired over the actual realization, over the paltry words which had to be assembled into long periods in order to capture the simplest things.

Never in the past nine years had I had the time or leisure to read the over eight hundred pages of my book at one go from start to finish; invariably I had got stuck after a few pages and had made amendments, because quite naturally I had, meanwhile, thought more thoroughly about problems, more intensively relived perceptions, and had altogether become a different person who wished to let his characters, too, benefit from those changes. However, emendations, elucidations of a written text are more difficult that the writing of the text itself, which is why most authors normally dispense with a revision and prefer to transfer their higher degree of knowledge – if such has arisen – to a new book. As, however, in no circumstances was I prepared to write a further book after the death of my hero, and indeed wanted this one to be regarded as my definitive testament, and as moreover I supported the belief that the hardest and most unusual thing was to hold death in check with a single book, I was time and again induced, while rejecting an all-through reading, to rework passages already finished. Now, however, after the decision on the hero's death, I could no longer be spared a continuous reading of the book, and I determined to see to it that the book was not, as it were, permeated by descriptions of thunderstorms, which, were this to be the case, I would exchange for a few sunny scenes, even if this altered the atmosphere of the hero's mental disposition.

With these poetological and formal problems of the writer's craft in my mind I finally reached the inn.

The taproom was overcrowded, and a thick obliterating veil of smoke hung over the tables covered with glasses and plates, round which young people were sitting so closely packed as if to make certain of their last meal ever. A strangely regular murmur filled the room, now and again broken by a burst of laughter, which abruptly came to an end. There were no transitions, no gradations, only the extreme forms of eruption and monotony. After a burst the heads would again bend over the food, but I had the impression that they were all only waiting to be allowed once more to jerk themselves back and up, impelled by a force whose source was unlikely to be found in the feeble stories that were being presented here: boastings, horror stories, seamen's yarns, as though we were living not in provincial Germany but in an exotic country beyond the sea. Standing in the door, dripping wet and with teeth chattering, I heard someone relate how Horst had been struck on the head by the boom, whereupon all of them performed the ritual of throwing back their heads, their mouths wide open, in which half-chewed food and stabbing tongues were mingling, only to snap forward again, ready for new commands. Only one man at the table, presumably Horst, had calmly gone on masticating and, with a full mouth, mumbled 'not true at all', a remark passed without further comment.

The stage management of my entrance was an utter failure. Despite the bizarre appearance which I must have presented no one took any notice of me, none of the numerous waitresses, all of whom I knew and who had frequently served me, made any attempt to assign me a seat, on the contrary, I was being pushed this way and that in order that the speciality of the establishment, roast pork, might be taken unobstructed to customers. These excesses of arrogance, which were silently acted out against me, making a nuisance out of a guest who was welcome enough during the week, one who often enough was the only diner among nothing but beer drinkers in the large taproom, made me realize to the full the misery of my existence. Among those present I, standing there, dripping, who had just taken a life-and-death decision, if not perpetrated a murder camouflaged as suicide, was of no account, this I could feel clearly, but in vain did I try to visualize a company which would have regarded me more highly or welcomed me more cordially. Only a few people knew me, and I had only revealed my narration project to people who neither had any conception of its dimensions nor any respect for writing, and if there was anyone left in this world who was able to interpret the intertwining threads of my meandering story as the only remaining form of expression for our present day, then that person was unknown to me. He certainly did not patronize this inn; among this sinister company of roast pork worshippers I would find no ally. On the other hand, this inn had over the past few years been the only place where I met anyone at all: from this murky pool I very largely drew my knowledge about the present, about the ruling spirit of the age, only here did I learn anything about newly invented words, political intrigues, cultural scandals, about the internal European market and the dramatic rise in disgust with politics. Here I learnt to my greatest amazement that a producer whose name was unfamiliar to me had come a cropper in Bremen with *A Winter's Tale*, moreover from a woman who, when questioned, had to admit to never having been to Bremen. Abstract processes of economic development were transformed at these tables into visually comprehensible occurrences by men who were either scarcely able to pay for their beer or stood on the other side, where nothing but percentages mattered. How often had I sat in this dimly lit room, filling page after page with what was being argued at the next table, verbosely or stutteringly, and if, on winter evenings, I was the only guest, I discussed the state of the world with the cook and his assistant, trying to bring some order into my table companions' muddled views on life. In vain, as it now turned out, for just that assistant, a cunning fellow from the north of Germany, from Lüneburg, a muscular show-off and braggart, now rammed me from behind with a full tray and passed me without greeting with calm indifferent gaze, without even acknowledging me.

Debased and humiliated I stood in a pool of water, which was already being lapped up by dogs, ill-behaved creatures which, panting, did not shrink from making my shoes too an object of their insatiability. As I did not wish to be accused of being unsociable I tried to put on a cheerful face and laughed out loud twice, but, apart from the dogs giving a start, achieved no effect whatever. I felt ill at ease, disregarded, an impression I could only refute by rigorous action. I therefore moved into the back room, where there was a cosy spot by a tiled stove, which I was especially fond of: one was almost unseen there but had a good view of the other tables and had the door in front of one, an old wooden door with wrought-iron fittings.

I nodded irresolutely to a girl who was sitting in my spot by the stove, staring at me fixedly, as if prepared to be thus perpetuated. Should I record this inexhaustible stare? Strictly speaking. I did not want to make any more notes: there was too great a danger that I could start filling up my *magnum opus* again which had only just undergone a brutal reduction. Observation ban, not observation increase was the self-appointed order of the hour. On the other hand, such unexpected discoveries should be noted down immediately because later on, during the writing process, they rarely presented themselves again. At my writing desk the girl's stare would become a normal stare, lost, dreamy, not quite conscious, sleepy-head-like, etc., whereas the stare of this woman seemed like a mask which she wore on her face to dispel evil spirits. There was a scene in my book which, after one glance at this masked woman, I would either have to delete or rewrite. The hero meets a girl whose stare, as it were, emits a beam that compels all persons passing through it to turn towards her. Only a completely distracted look, total absence of deliberation, could pass through that glance barrier unaffected, everyone else, including my hero, had to gaze into the Medusa's eye. I had developed this scene into a little story in order to conclude a long theoretical chapter on aesthetic problems with a divertimento. The model for it was a girl from my form, a totally empty person who possessed nothing except that look, with which she was able, scantily, to fill her emptiness. When she was by herself everything within her collapsed, and she was therefore compelled to hang about public places, after school by preference at railway stations, and it was at a railway station that I had met her again. I had noticed that all those hurrying figures suddenly halted or at least slowed down their pace at a particular spot, looking towards one of the mushroom-shaped beer tables by which the staring girl was standing, indeed a few steps further on several of them once more turned their heads, re-assuring themselves with astonishment that for a moment they had actually been interrupted in their purposeful movement, which resulted in the most splendid collisions. I had sneaked up to my ex-classmate from behind and placed myself with a beer obliquely at her side in order accurately to explore the effect of her gaze, but was soon tracked down by the person I had come to meet, who now, coming from the platforms and loaded with baggage, was staggering in our direction, straight into the sightline of the girl. He stopped by my classmate's side and put down his cases as if intending to stay near her, but she had drained her glass and moved off in triumph, head held high. In my manuscript I had transposed the scene to another arena and assigned to it the function of making clear to the hero the necessity of bounds and limitations, so that his gaze – the modern gaze, as I hoped – should not lose itself or fritter itself away aimlessly but be deliberately concentrated. The hero forces himself to patronize a certain restaurant increasingly frequently, where there is a waitress with just that kind of look, which must inevitably fall upon him several times during an evening. In the manner of the classics I had described how the hero imagines that this look was death, and the test consisted of standing up to that look of death, so that afterwards he would see everything through different eyes. Paradoxically, however, the waitress misinterprets the eyes which are constantly on her, that contest of glances, not as a ritual of warding off death but as an invitation, which leads to a very comical union: when eventually they share a bed they keep calling out to each other to shut their eyes.

As I was now looking into the eyes of the staring girl in the smoke-filled back room of the inn I wanted to turn back at once in order to revise the relevant chapter of my book: death is the sum-total of all our lives, we must not let ourselves be looked at, but the erupting thunderstorm outside prevented me from leaving. Shakily I sat down at the next table, where the proprietor of the local live-cell sanatorium was having his dinner: a man with whom I was very well acquainted though I did not much like him, who, for an unbelievable – to a writer an astronomical – fee had bought himself the title of professor from a South-American sham university. The case had been reported in the press, which neither prevented his patients from having themselves injected by him nor himself from telling the story boastfully and without any sense of wrong, as he held the (probably not entirely mistaken) view that present-day lawfully acquired professorial titles were based on far lesser achievements than his own life's work in the live-cells field. Look at those grey moulds back there at the corner table, he called out to me cheerfully, they've arrived today: in a week they'll be dancing on the tables here. Even though that was hardly to be expected – the persons referred to were an elderly couple – I had certainly noticed the effect which his therapy had on the patients who often strolled past my house, and I had more than once been inclined to overcome my reservations and put myself in the hands of this ruffian to be rejuvenated after many years of servitude at my desk. But one glance at his hands, clenched into fists, led me to other thoughts, and while the professor was loudly talking away to a third guest at our table I had an opportunity to order a beer and a chive sandwich.

The pale third man did not leave me the necessary quiet to play through different chapter stories in my head, as I had intended: whenever I had got to a sensitive point, from the realization of which I expected structural improvements, he would cut through my reflections with his nasal dicton. And the subject of his talk provided ample cause for all kinds of diversions, because this unimpressive gentleman was no less than the doyen of leech research. He had spent years over the unsolved problem of why a creature weighing about two grammes takes on roughly ten grammes of mammal blood only once every year or two, of which it again excretes as much as 60 per cent after only eight hours, i.e. the water and salt constituents, and nevertheless leads something like an orderly life. The problem of the physiological regulatory system which keeps the salt-water balance of the small creatures constant even under stress had been solved by our table companion. He had discovered receptors which recorded the blood concentration and the blood volume, reporting any changes to the central nervous system, which in turn instructs the nephridia – the excretory organs, as he informed us in a whisper – to increase their water and salt discharge in such a way that the former blood concentration and the former blood volume are restored again within a few hours.

Scarcely credible, said the professor, and I would have said something similar if I were not thereby putting myself on the same level as the ruffian. But I was fascinated by the idea that, like a leech, I might only have to visit the ghastly inn once every few years in order, subsequently, to digest quietly for the next twelve months. Many problems of coexistence would be solved at a stroke if it were possible to fit the leech's ionic pumps into the human organism, I remarked timidly, which induced the leech researcher, who was no fool at all, to embark on a longish discourse about the possible utilization of his discovery, which, putting it mildly, contained near-fascist elements. All of a sudden he saw his opportunity to present us with his theory of man and his degeneration, and I was simply amazed to hear this pale dwarf now uttering views which, in a democratically constituted society, would deserve to be severely prosecuted. Suddenly the leech was the superior creature, its physiological organization preferable to that of man, and it would not have taken much for him to declare the black bloodsucker to be the crown of creation, whereas man, on that ladder, was steadily approaching his decline.

It was of course nothing new to me – and I had also referred to it in my book – that a certain type of scientist, especially those who continually peered down their microscopes, was inclined to place the wedding dance of the bee above the achievements of the Bolshoi Ballet, but that a leech in its brackish water should come out top in comparison with human culture – that, even I felt, was going too far, especially as the live-cells professor was agreeing noisily with every absurd remark of the researcher and eventually, as the bottom line of our conversation, declared that live-cell therapy and leeching were the sole achievements of the human intellect worthy of mention and which, in a Germany reunited within proper frontiers, would have to assume the leading role in education.

We had not, to put it conservatively, left the beer idle in its barrels, with the result that our argument had altogether left the rails of scientific discussion; however, I had the uncomfortable feeling of having landed in the wrong company. A cautious look around me told me that all the guests of the small back room were in fact listening to the pale researcher's escapades with expressions of disgust. But before I was able, by a certain miming, to convey that I did not by any means associate myself with these two inflamed gentlemen, I was called to order by a violent thump on my shoulder by the professor. You're a damned pessimist, he boomed into my ear and thumped me once more, so that the beer from the glass which I had raised in defence splashed over my shirt, a pessimist inclined equally towards anarchy and melancholia. Pessimist evidently was a term of contempt to this man, while I associated the sweetest ideas with it. My favourite chapter in the book was about an argument between my hero and a pessimist, which I had written during a long winter in northern Mexico years ago. In the morning, before work, I used to read a page of Ludwig Wittgenstein's *Miscellaneous Reflections*, in the evening, after work, the novels of Alejo Carpentier, and during the day I would touch up the argument with the profound and maybe a little too highly educated pessimist, into whose mouth I placed page after page in order to prove the pointlessness of human action, until eventually, in a bar in New York, he was allowed to triumph over my resigned hero. Maybe you are right, was his last sentence, but there is absolutely nothing a pessimist can prove. Those were the most intensive writing months of my life, never was I happier than at that time.

The money for the journey I had earned by a job as a packer in a publishing firm. Within a few days I had noticed that the stock of available books was not decreasing, although we – a Turk, a Sudeten German and myself – spent eight hours each day packing books and dispatching them. In a lengthy internal memo I reported this, to my mind managerially deplorable, state of affairs and was promptly asked up to the first floor of the villa, where the head of the firm, a stocky German scholar of the Bonn school, along with two secretaries and a publisher's reader were responsible for the contents of the books we had to dispatch. The head of the firm had a varying relationship with the two women, and whenever his urge was focusing more on one of them, the publisher's reader had to look after the other. This was doing him no good, as was plain to anybody, and the books, too, suffered from this intercourse because they went to the printer for the most part unread.

I related my observations of the unchanging number of books in stock and also admitted to some packing errors committed by the Sudeten German, who, unlike the Turk, had no command, or only a gappy one, of the language of the books, without the result being essentially changed. There is a lot of activity in the packing department, I summed up the first part of my report, but when the number of books dispatched more or less equals that of books returned stocking capacity, given continuing production, would soon be exhausted. Much action, no sales. Basically the only copies not returned were the free copies, sent out to enable journalists to complete their private libraries, but even that could not be relied upon because many recipients of these gifts were selling the books unopened to the local book trade at half price, which then returned them to the publishers. So as not to seem a sourpuss, moreover one not trained in the business, I made a proposal which was instantly accepted with applause: every other manuscript recommended for acceptance should be turned down.

The success was so striking that the Turk had to be dismissed because there was not enough work, whereas I received a salary increase. And a few months later all that was being published were pornographic novels by women living in Austria, brought across the frontier under the label of 'feminine aesthetics', which found a few customers because the charm of once more hearing all those fine old pornographic words from Austrian women's lips was irresistible. The rest – lyrical protrayals of the summer months, travel accounts and first-person-singular novels in which the world and human activities were presented in a tragic perspective – were no longer published. The authors of such works would occasionally turn up in our basement, jovial lads and care-worn women, stand us a beer and look in amazement at the full shelves, their own future destiny. Fuck-novel or first-person-singular, the Sudeten German would ask them in his obliging way, putting his thumb between two fingers, and if the answer was in the direction of a tragic view of the world he would let his thumb hang down. If we felt sorry for them we would, in the lunchbreak, write a massive figure three at the start of the manuscript, knowing that the publisher's reader rarely got beyond the first page, and thus we helped many an author into publication, even if reviews then criticized the misproportion between the crudely sexual start and the lyrical-meditative remainder of the novel. At any rate, the enterprise enjoyed a fierce if short-lived boom, only to collapse just as fiercely afterwards. The head of the publishing house tried for a while to keep above water by the sale of winter campfires to neo-fascist marginal groups, but soon went over to alcohol and fossilized. By way of compensation the publisher's reader, the women secretaries, the Sudeten German and I each received, apart from two artificial camp-fires, a portion of the stock of novels, which I was later able, with a suitable discount, to sell to a lover of Austrian literature. After my return from Mexico, with the fiery pessimism chapter down on paper, I was occasionally visited by the publisher's reader who wanted to avail himself of my managerial know-how to set up a new publisher's bookshop, but none of the publication projects proposed by him, all of them devoted to the subject of body experience and philosophy, in other words a higher form of pornography, seemed to me of a kind that would make me wish to renew business relations with him. This new Berlin Body School is a goldmine once we have the right marketing concept, he tried to bait me, but I had already waved it aside with a weary gesture.

I was reminded of that happy time of my life as the live-cells professor now called me a pessimist. Whether it was out of respect for the man's age or of shame at voluntarily keeping company with such a person, I did not insist on correcting that statement but confined myself to a grunt, and the ensuing discussion between the professor and the leech researcher about the steady spread of pessimism likewise had to manage without any contribution from me. The waitresses meanwhile had stood the chairs on the tables, and we alone were still sitting there in our small circle, drinking beer and now and again a schnapps to make sure the intensity of the conversation did not flag. The cook and his assistant had also joined us: grinning they sat there, their tall hats before them. No doubt you're the loser, the assistant said to me; he was a man who did not understand anything and even lacked the basic skills of his own trade. You shut up, said the cook, whose friendship I could have easily done without in the past. Someone's got to be the loser, the assistant pouted, so why not the pessimist, and while saying so he let his blotchy tongue sweep across his lips. I told you to shut up, the cook repeated in monosyllables, you're a damned pessimist yourself. Thus one word led to another and escalated into a conversation now also supported by the waitresses. I like pessimists, one of the waitresses chipped in, a limp woman whom one might not indeed have expected to support even the most miserable optimist. Pessimists are more interesting than optimists, she summed up her views, confirming them with a wink in my direction.

At daybreak we set out for home, arms linked: the leech researcher was hanging from the arm of the professor, who had put his other arm round me, I had seized the waitress round her hip, while the assistant cook hung limply on the waitress's free hand. Without aiming out steps we staggered up the hill, the cook in the rear, his white hat at odds with the surroundings. With brief interruptions – the leech researcher had to puke, the professor to draw some deep breaths, the waitress to drag the assistant cook's hands out from her waist-band and the cook to close up with us – we stumbled briskly ahead and suddenly found ourselves in front of my abode, whose mottled timber, lightly covered with dew, was suffused by a warm light from the first rays of the sun. It looked Russian, confidence-inspiring, revealing nothing of the drama it concealed. The chef and his assistant slid to the ground back to back and instantly fell asleep, the professor settled down in the shed behind the tractor, the leech researcher, with a green hue, knelt down in front of the toilet, and I lay down with the waitress on the pull-out couch and listened to *Harold* by Berlioz, a kind of music which silenced the waitress on the spot. I therefore had some quiet in which to order my jumbled thoughts, with the result that about the hour of nine I freed myself from the downy arms of Eva – that was her name – tiptoed over to my manuscript, took out the big chapter about the pessimist, nearly eighty pages of it, stepped outside my chalet, cast a glance at the chef who had now keeled over, heard the muttered groans of the leech researcher through the lavatory window and grimly acknowledged the snores of the professor, and eventually ran down to the meadow, where, under the curious glances of my faithful friends the brown cows, I burnt the convolute of fiercely resisting pages. My views on pessimism had been defiled, now they were to regain their primordial purity in the quickly leaping flames. Over the past twenty hours I had deprived my public of roughly three hundred pages of my originally over-eight-hundred-pages-long manuscript, an action which filled me with pride, satisfaction and profound anxiety.

8

Towards midday a local gendarmerie car eventually turned up to look for the professor who had been reported missing. I handed him over without protest. As the police evidently had reason to show gratitude to him they carefully pulled him out by his legs from underneath the tractor and bedded him down on newspapers in the back of their station wagon, where this lamentable figure rolled up like a wounded animal, groaning, pulling his oil-stained jacket over his head and remaining motionless. The two cooks were shoved, rather less gently, on to the back seat, where they bounced into one another stupidly, then the windows were lowered to let fresh air blow over the ill-smelling company, and the car would have driven off had I not, yelling loudly, pointed to the lavatory, where the leech researcher, meanwhile turned yellow and generally conveying the impression of wishing to adopt the shape of his research objects, was still, covered in vomit from top to bottom, hanging on in front of the cracked porcelain bowl.

Even the trained police officers had to scratch their brains for a while before hitting on the trick of dragging the stiff gentleman through the narrow door, during which his trousers parted company with his skinny behind and remained hanging, an unappetizing bundle, above his ankles. Not a sight for the German research community, I thought to myself, but made no effort to lend a hand: too deep sat the sting of affront, too pure was my contempt for people of his type, who were allowed, in the name of research and teaching, to sully the face of reason. Outside, the man was unfolded and pulled lengthwise across the knees of the cooks, head downwards. Fucking pessimist, were the first words I heard from one member of that disparate band of brothers, and they remained the only ones. I had to give a written assurance to the policemen that I would not leave the country until this incident had been cleared up, whereupon the heavily laden vehicle departed, its blue light flashing.

Thus I stood shivering in the early sunshine, gazing down on the lake which, grey and indolent, was awaiting the day, yet I was somehow relieved to have come out of this adventure with my skin saved. The manuscript had suffered, certainly, and yet the loss of the one chapter seemed to me bearable, indeed necessary, in order to keep the rest free of all conceivable philosophically coloured accusations. Just because of the conclusion of the book, of the unexpected suicide, any allusion to motives had to be avoided on the preceding pages, and the pessimism chapter especially might have induced a non-talented reviewer to see in it the reason for the hero's suicide. Lapses of taste of this kind occurred time and again because many reviewers, by their insensitive cleverness, were inclined to examine books and lives as to their consistency, and, in the absence of proof of casual explanations, to accept the incompatible as entirely compatible. This observation applies more particularly to books which end with a death, because most people evidently need a conclusive explanation for death, beyond all aesthetic and literary problems that may be raised by it.

A butterfly was sitting motionless on the backrest of my chair; it would be a warm day. Inwardly I was now sufficiently settled to get out my manuscript and embark on reworking it, for even though, after the voluminous elimination of chapters over the past few hours, there would now be less work, there was still quite enough left. But just as if I had loudly proclaimed that I would devote this day to idleness, the door opened and discharged the waitress. The fine down on her body was lending her figure a kind of saintly halo, which was totally at variance with her character, which could, more or less accurately, be described as unsaintly. At any rate, she sat down heavily on my lap, wrapped her soft arms around my head and laid her forehead on my shoulders, so that my sensitive nose had to come to rest in her smoke-perfumed hair, and if my legs had not just then gone to sleep she would have done. As it was, I had to get up and deposit the heavy white body in the meadow, where at first it remained lying like a block of granite.

Work was out of the question: her flesh was flashing too obscenely through the green blades, distracting my eyes from chapter one. What could be done about that woman who was making no move to leave my property? There was nothing left but to address her, but any reasonable allocution only produced a feebly mumbled echo. You're crushing the grass, you're ruining the dandelion clocks, I called out to her, you're spoiling the look of the landscape, you're disturbing the harmony, the ants will bite you – nothing induced the self-willed creature to remedy the intolerable situation. Eventually, to calm my eyes, I got the blanket from my couch and laid it over the girl, who, the moment my shadow fell on her, spread out her arms and opened her mouth as if, after all that silence, she was at last about to suggest a solution. I therefore bent down and placed my ear against her lips but was immediately grabbed and drawn under the blanket. She was, as I instantly realized, stronger than me, in spite of all so-called femininity, which was why, after initial resistance, I yielded and, with eyes firmly shut, became a witness to the most depraved operations. Stop it, I begged, we don't even know each other, but such pleas did not seem to move her. I tried desperately to think of something else, in order at least inwardly to remain pure, but nothing I could think of could equal that primal urge. Should I change my book from the first person singular to the third person singular? Should I really improve, smoothe out, the rough and crude chapters, especially at the beginning, or should I leave them as they were, in order to emphasize the coincidental from which my hero was shaping his life? Should I give him an occupation, a firmly circumscribed activity, a regular daily routine, in order to move the deviations, especially of his intellect, more strongly and more clearly into the foreground? Should I not incorporate some perspective even in the first chapter? It occurred to me that an interment at the opening might be a dramatic peg, the interment of his mother for instance? My own prolonged solitude had led me to leave the man sitting simply in his room, which had created a complicity that possibly benefited me but not necessarily the manuscript. He must get out and about, I shouted at the waitress, who was laboriously pursuing her activity, he must move around, he must have friends about him, from whom he can detach himself, I shall send him to parties, he must get to know other strata of society, other races, women must impart the primal facets of life to him. The alarmed cheerfulness which I had lent my voice caused the girl to stop. I want to work, I have to work, and nothing on earth shall prevent me from accomplishing my work, I said relieved, as if freed from a nightmare, when once more I had firm ground under my feet.

She stayed. I sat under the sun umbrella at my table and vainly tried to add a little worldliness to my hero, in subordinate clauses, to make sure the main structure did not totter, while she ran around the garden stark naked, talking to herself. When the first walkers stopped, glued to the fence, enthralled by that ludicrous performance, she tied on an apron she had found in the woodshed, a blue bib-apron, with the ambiguous effect that the first holiday visitor asked from the fence whether we had rooms to let in this house. We're full up, she called back with a cheerful wave, come back tomorrow, and with these words she turned her bare back on them. I was getting seriously worried about my work, for by the afternoon, as the sun was beginning to go down, I had just managed one page of shaky writing, and to my deepest despair my emendations consisted of my having deleted a whole page and compressed it into a single sentence, a sentence moverover which, in its casualness, contained no hint of the splendour to be spread out on the succeeding pages. What had become of the haughty constructions, where were the linguistic echoes which were hiding in all the parentheses and brackets in order to unfold their full sonority the moment the reading eye fell upon them? Why had I sacrificed in a single afternoon what for many years had seemed to me the most inspired entry in my meandering work? Was the woman the cause of this bookkeeperish destructiveness, the naked woman who, not being directly addressed by anyone, had meanwhile retired to the couch again? With dismay I read the few lines which, squeezed into the margin as if they, too, had no justification for being on the paper, now seemed like a bad joke by comparison to the structure they were to replace: 'Grown out of the mirage of my high-flying dreams, I attempted, in the spirit of absolute subjectivity, to discover the truth about my weakening sense of what makes the world hang together, without mourning the loss of the luxuriant wilderness of my evanescent identity.' Was this the opening of a novel, of a cosmic drama?

Were such sentences capable of startling a readership that had schooled their perceptions on all those *petit-bourgeois* matrimonial dramas and social tearjerkers, or of stirring an expectation which would darken their brightly polished horizon at a blow? Was the purity and sincerity of self-questioning clear enough in those lines? I could feel the tears jerking into my eyes and had to summon up and rally all my remaining courage in order to complete with dignity what had to be completed: I took the whole of chapter one from the pile and, with loud lamentations, tore it up into minute snippets which, crying and sobbing, I surrendered to a mercifully descending wind.

9

One day Karl – I realized of course that this could not remain his final name – received an invitation to a dinner party at the house of the son of an industrialist (specify), who had a seat on the board of his father's firm, and, contrary to his custom of declining all such diversions, accepted because the dinner was being given in honour of some young artists whose show at the local artists' club had caused some excitement. The young host, younger than Karl and, as was to emerge, extremely well versed in matters concerning modern art, had not only made the young artists' show possible but had, even before its opening raised it to the rank of an event by purchasing several large canvases. After the soup (possibly to be replaced by another dish: *vitello tonnato* or suchlike) he gave a short welcoming address which provided excellent proof of his stupendous knowledge and of his taste: the artist, he said, is the last person immune against institutions, the only person capable of resisting the functional powers whose victims we all are – and I do not exclude myself. And it is he – why shouldn't we speak about it, he asked a rhetorical question – who thrives and resides in the immediate proximity of power. This was so at the time of the Renaissance (examples, names), and nothing has changed in this respect since: art and power are twins, man and woman, with power, money, the male principle being the immobile element and art, the female principle, being the mobile element. Power needs beauty, and that is also the reason why I should like to call out to all those chicken-hearted industrialists, who shun art and do not buy pictures, who are afraid of getting a taste of the exalted (better the sublime): Face up to beauty, only beauty can save you! (Save perhaps too strong.) Karl could see in the faces of the young artists how the prices of their pictures were climbing, and he was not therefore surprised when the four young men who were sitting opposite him and who during the soup (see above) had been discussing the advantageous purchase of villas in Spain, burst into cheers when the young host came to an end. Spot on, one of them said, absolutely spot on, the bit about the sublime, quite fantastic. (Possibly a more modish word: fab, etc.)

My husband likes equilibrating between extremes, the host's wife said to Karl who sat next to her, and if he didn't have to take over the firm he would have become a painter, an abstract painter I suppose, detached from vile reality, because it is his nature to love any form of ecstasy, intoxication, excitement, eruption, madness. When one sees him like this, in a suit, she whispered to him, one wouldn't believe the excesses of revelation, of self-discardment, he is capable of, a psychopath and a dreamer, closer to infantilism than to reason, who needs his residual intellect as a powerful corrective against the apparations and visions which haunt him. I know those states of excitement which come upon him at the sight of modern art, his loss of commonsense that goes hand in hand with his purchase of paintings, he no longer knows me then, all he sees is colour. Our marriage would be a story of disintegration if the firm (important: nature of the firm) did not time and again bring him back to his senses, a story of degeneration, a pure masque. The meal was over, coffee and liqueurs were being served, in which Karl – quite unlike the now merry painters who were making aeroplanes out of their napkins and launching them into the *décolletage* of his other neighbour, the wife of the sales manager, who was also interested in modern art – did not indulge much. He felt ill at ease amidst all those commonplaces which were here being traded as philosophy, he was disgusted by the shrinking of competence, by the absence of a sense of propriety, so that he was glad when their host sat down on the vacated chair of the sales manager's wife, who for her part had expressed the wish to be instructed, in a quiet room, by one of the painters on the movements of inspiration (too strong ?). To Karl's delight their host revealed himself as a wholly competent person, who was able to explain to him, accurately and without beating about the bush, the problems of the metal industry (not plastics, after all ?), to discuss raw material and marketing problems with business-like clarity and generally to convey a more lucid picture of his occupation than Karl would have credited any of the painters present with providing of their occupation. You should write an epic of the metal-working industry, Karl said, the novel of raw material shortages, but their host modestly (wearily, weakly, reference to his unstable constitution?) shrugged off the suggestion. That he would rather leave to the artists, he said, with them one wasn't sure when they were poking fun and when they were being serious, and their moral alienation was so total that they really believed they had to add one more picture to great art. I'm only staging this whole performance for the entertainment of my slightly eccentric wife, he added (whispered to him), whose pure lack of knowledge induces her to surround herself with ever new paintings. She lacks a purpose in her life, her responsibility is used up, she has no mission, he said cheerfully, hence this system of compensation. She no longer sees the losses which we still see, she has no feeling for losses (develop the categories of loss!). Hence also her inability to read a book, a tragedy.

Thus they continued their conversation for quite a while, until the heir had to call an ambulance because the sales manager's wife had had a fainting fit in connection with her instruction by the painter and sculptor. She was looked after, half undressed, in the drawing room, and admired, and eventually taken to hospital by two sturdy young ambulance men.

Karl did not stay much beyond midnight.

Cross out everything. No more satire. Into the dustbin with it.

10

The time had come to face facts. After all, the work of approximately three years had been undone in little more than two days, an achievement totally out of proportion and one which made me fear the worst for the subsequent chapters and hence for my future. The manuscript now looked slim, schoolboyishly unready, miserable, and scarcely able ever to fill two book covers. I was reminded of the time when I had declared myself sufficiently mature to embark on writing down the final version. Then, too, it had been summer, a gossamer summer full of whitethorn and bugbane, whose ramified inflorescences and bursting seedpods had then taken up almost more of my time than the demonstrations against everything and everybody not holding the opinions we did. I was then far more concerned with the question of whether the broader concept of species of Huth (1883) and later of Ascherson and Graeber (1929) was still justified or whether the different varieties of Actaea should not after all be treated as species in their own right, a far-reaching set of problems in systematic botany, which I, to the irritation of my companions, was fond also of applying to social problems. But one day I got fed up with looking for material for a doctoral thesis in the dusty drawers of central-European flora research, and I felt I would rather go through life without an academic degree than further delay the writing of my true life's work. So I severed all ties which bound me to a student's life and embarked on the nearly ten years of preparatory searching for material, which preceded another nearly ten years of actually writing my manuscript.

A strange period. Moments of deep depression alternated with periods full of confidence that I would bring my project of a novel-like history of imagination, illustrated by the example of a heroic eccentric, to a successful conclusion, being reassured in my enterprise by occasional sideways glances into the topical literature: dry, uninspired and boring; and malicious and mean though the treatment of the problem in philosophical literature may have been, it has not been a subject of *belles lettres*, which persistently had been giving the topic a wide berth, and had moreover, by its crazy moving in circles, removed itself totally beyond the interest of humanity. During the preliminary work I was feeling increasingly that I was, as a solitary individual, confronting the central problem of the present age, a problem which was snarling at me with a thousand tongues. The nineteenth century had gone into my notebooks, Schopenhauer was excerpted and Kierkegaard totally frittered away, the soul emerged on the empty horizon of the turn of the century and found an entry into countless notebooks of mine, the battles of material of the First World War and fascism in all its facets, finally the decline of imagination in the Second Word War and its clumsy faking up during the post-war period as art and trash. History was at an end, my novel could begin.

In a sea captain's house on the Turkish coast, which a friend from my university days let me use for a year free of charge, especially as in its immediate neighbourhood the military of the Junta had set up a firing range, I drafted my structures and diagrams, operational ensembles and experimental groupings to gain control over the chaos of my notes. What I had to avoid at all costs was letting my book become a learned historical botch, a theoretical treatise on the dying away of imagination, its ebbing away, its petering out, which would inescapably have placed this work within the horizon of decadence and decline, of self-pity and apathy that was beginning to grow around me. Upon large white sheets of paper I had written orders to myself and pinned them to the outside walls of the sea captain's house: Against the immanence of the system! Against psychologism and the angst cult! Against non-relating! One evening a delegation of the garrison had turned up, led by an officer who had worked at Siemens in Munich and spoke tolerable German, in order to arrange for the removal of my white flags. However, as a polite Turk he wished to know what was written on those banners and what I was trying to say with them. Self-discipline, I informed him, these banners are orders for self-discipline, to make sure my art did not become the object of a capitalist decorative epidemic, of all those disquisitions on injustice, which, in an age of indifference to everything evident sucked in the authentic and only allowed trans-semiotic mental models of post-conceptualism – that was the meaning of those mementoes. The delegation withdrew to the garden, where the officer translated for them my elucidation of the white flags, or tried to translate it, because he kept running back into the house for more precise explanations of concepts unfamiliar in Turkish military circles. Especially the indifference to everything evident made him despair. If I am evident, I belong to the realm of the evident, is Turkey part of the realm of the evident, is Greece, is nature, the goat in front of your house? It turned into a long evening, an evening of instruction, of eager learning, of exchange, and when eventually a barrel of wine was delivered by a courier called up by radio, the soldiers could scarcely contain themselves: coherence lies, they said in chorus, down with the slogan of the immaterial, they called out to each other, until an icy wind from Anatolia put an end to the aesthetic discussion. My white sheets danced and swirled above the house and were carried off to sea, tiny little points in a vast blue sky which tore up my commands with a cold mien and swallowed them. What a year! And at the end of it I left the Junta behind me and returned to Germany, where, in a sheltered spot, I began to write the first chapter, the one that was now expunged, torn up, shredded, extinguished.

The enormous deception of human existence, which was to be portrayed in my book, would collapse into a harmless lie unless an up-wind once more mobilized my forces. Eva came out of the house, dressed, and with shoes on her feet. Over her black blouse she had put on my only jacket, its sleeves rolled up. See you soon, she said, and I turned pale. She had evidently decided to stay, to narrow my bed, to shorten my working time. And if she persevered with her practice of rape she would also weaken my body. As if she had guessed my thoughts she promised to bring me back something to make me strong, left-overs, so you regain your strength, and so saying she winked at me frivolously with her left eye, viciously enjoying my alarm. Until what time are you on duty, I asked drily. As long as you like, she purred. What I wanted to know was when you'll be back. Soon. And you work hard, she reminded me amidst kisses, you finish your fat little book so we get rich and can travel round the world, and so saying she cheekily shot her tongue into my ear and pawed my fear-rigid body, which no longer seemed to belong to me at all. And then she was suddenly out in the meadow, on the hill among the cows, waving and shouting some obscene words or other in my direction, and finally vanishing from sight.

11

Alone again, I removed from my manuscript all the passages I had written with unswerving loyalty to the power of love as the motor of imagination. These came to more than sixty pages, three complete chapters and many smaller sections, which I did not simply cross out but carefully excised whenever the rest of the page contained any usable ideas, ideas necessary for the continuity of the storyline. With the fluttering and obstinate pages I went down to the lake and, confirmed in the knowledge that I was doing the right thing at the right time, I drowned them. Slowly the ink began to dissolve and to mingle with the water in small slicks. Curious little fish swam up, nudged the ever cleaner pages and turned away again. Like jellyfish the sheets adjusted to the waves, drifted to the shore and were carried out again. I must have crouched like this by the water for about an hour, proud and sad, with insects swarming about me, then I rose to my feet, lightly raised my hand and returned to the house.

The earth was steaming. Empty and dejected, as if walking towards an abyss, I shuffled along the gravel path which gleamed at unexpected spots in the pale evening light. There was a smell of damp wood and of cow dung. I had perceived all those smells and smell mixtures so often that I felt ashamed of perceiving them like that and not differently. The thought that in my book someone, having just annihilated a vital document, might be walking along a gravel path, noting that the earth was steaming and that there was a smell of damp wood and cow dung definitely caused my mood to collapse. Probably the person whose crunching steps I could hear on the gravel behind me also perceived nothing different. Probably that person had just noticed how beautifully the earth was steaming and what an aromatic smell there was of damp wood and cow dung. I felt superfluous, as if no longer existing, and if my increasingly ludicrous anxiety about my book had not been nagging me I would have crumbled into myself like an over-rotten fungus. This book, whose hero had already heard his death sentence, kept me, wriggling, alive. But the thread binding words, objects and ideas to me had become so thin, so frayed and worn that I feared it might snap, suddenly, here on my way, snap with a twanging sound and leave me behind, without support. Perhaps I would have to wait with the revision of the remaining parts of my manuscript for a new solidity to have formed within me, a practically effective energy that would release the hard kernel from the quarry of emptied fragments within me, the kernel which would repay chiselling into shape.

At the moment, however, I was unable to imagine from what dark corner of the crumbling structure of my life, that artificial ruin, help should arrive for me. Someone totally supporting himself on an idea, on a work, moreover a work about imagination, has no firm foothold in this world once the idea begins to break up at one point, there is no ancillary hold, let alone in human beings. I was that work, that work was me, both were crumbling, and this depressing discovery was not helped by any cynicism, by any contrived gaiety, by any vitalism in the shape of Eva. I was a serpent biting its own tail, and only I could feel the pain and the hoplessness. As I was thus groping my way towards my old house, totally lost, a fiery hatred suddenly arose in me, out of the midst of depression there sprang a hate-flower, luxuriating upwards and almost taking my breath away. I had to stop and control myself, but the hatred was stronger and burst out of me in a wild verbal orgy. Leave me alone, I screamed at the blue sky above the lake, leave me in peace, you sorry philosophers, restore my tranquillity, people, I want to go back into myself and meet myself there, without pity, without encouragement, without interference. Banish sentiments, banish the small universe of deception, you belong to the outside world with your indestructible butchers' humaneness, and so on and so on, all disjointed fragments, but cumulatively they nevertheless produced something like a weapon with which, at least for a short while, I might keep life at arm's length. For too long, it seemed, I had pursued the idea of purity for me to be now suddenly pierced to the heart by impurity. To the heart? To the guts, this cry came from my guts, where the ideas are still stuck in the primeval mire. The sight of the house calmed me, only a shiver remained, a grumbling afterquake, a thinning of the blood, and my tongue was, quivering, drooping over my lower lip. What had become of my work, by which I had hoped to lend a massive structure to the paralysing impotence of my life? What remained of my intention quietly to construct that edifice as a strict mental exercise, in order to provide a clear confrontation to the dimness and vagueness that surrounded me, covering the heads of my contemporaries with a repulsive veil? Where now was my long nurtured hope of accumulating, in my solitude, an inner energy which would enable me, without any opposition, without any dependence or tactical consideration, to accomplish my work? And what had become of my conviction that my plan could be executed only by the strictest respect for rules, the infringement of which would mean rupture? My work was to have been a final summing up, and it was to have managed without the irony which spoiled all the literary efforts of our day. Anything contemporary was to have been eliminated, had to be eliminated, whenever it tried to emerge at the level of description, anything political, anything historical, in short: none of the experiences I found described in nearly every book was to have passed my pen. And what had happened? Had I too not written one of those ridiculous pieces of fiction which are invented every day, written up, sold and read, for the sole purpose of making money, enjoying a reputation, wielding power? Writing a novel was in any case a business for dubious minds which had to fit their few ideas into a framework since otherwise they would be lost in the night of history. And all those descriptions of nocturnal gravel paths and quiet lakes, of the smells of wood and cowshit, all this fuss about allegedly affected souls in affected circumstances was so distasteful and mindless, so vile and coarse that their producers naturally enjoyed a reputation in a society which had lost the skill of story-telling, whose imagination was atrophied and whose capacity for thought was below the perception level admissible a mere hundred years ago. To that type of person irony was of course closer than any other intellectual agility. Not a single page of my book, I had firmly resolved during those ten years, should exude the poisonous stench of coquetry or vanity, the infamous glitter of banal artistic *naïveté* which issued from virtually all the writing that I came across at the time, the tormenting dullness of the sociological mode of thinking that was being hailed as the prime truth.

And now? I was no longer sure what I had actually written. Do I have to start all over again, I anxiously asked the lake which was indifferently murmuring its prayers as though it knew the sinister shapes which were trying, excitedly, to provoke an answer from it.

12

I must have fallen asleep, for as I raised my head from my painful lower arms and opened my eyes, Eva and a stranger were standing before me in the room. To call my mood bad would have been base flattery, but it dropped below the limit of what even I was prepared to put up with when the young gentleman, who had introduced himself too unclearly for me safely to repeat his name, in a challenging voice asked to see my manuscript. Is it that thing over there, he said, pointing to what was most sacred to me, and as my crushed mental condition prevented me from answering and as, moreover, there was no other manuscript within sight, he pulled my manuscript out from under my protective arms, sat down straddle-legged on the couch and began to read. Who is he, I asked Eva who had joined me and who was feeding me leftovers from the inn, which she had brought back with her, cold kidneys, fatty entrails of chickens, innards of such penetrating smell that even the reading stranger began to turn up his nose, carrot stumps and finally bits of food which the guests had been quite justified in leaving uneaten on their plates, but which I had to take into my mouth. Who is he, I asked more loudly, with the result that a large portion of the food spilled on to the lap of my new girlfriend, who, however, did not protest. On the contrary, her affection for me seemed to be of a genuine nature, because she carefully collected everything and shoved it, now in smaller, more easily chewable helpings, back into my mouth. Eat up first, she said cheerfully, then we'll see, a statement whose unashamed motherliness robbed me of the rest of my self-control. I slid to the ground, well-nigh unconscious, and Eva let it happen, indeed she lay down by my side and in this position quite seriously began softly to sing a love song, a hit of the most mawkish kind, which, however, had one good point: after the fifth or sixth of its unending stanzas the rhymes gave out. After that the tune broke up into small, only breathed, fragments, and finally Eva fell asleep. I sorted out our legs, got up, and stepped over to the reader, but winced and refrained from snatching the manuscript from him, as I had intended, because on his rough blotchy face, which did not seem to match his neat clothes at all, there was an air of most profound harmony. And seeing that, though an impertinent intruder, he nevertheless was, after me, the first reader of my work, I sank back again in silence on a chair, in an observant attitude, my hands carefully placed on my knees. The man facing me, who was evidently encouraged in his dicourteous behaviour by the quality of my work, calmly turned one page after another, now and again frowned or uttered a soundless laugh, seized his hair, plucked his lip and tore off several bits of skin, which he carelessly flicked into the room, scratched his ankle and generally acted as if I had requested him to read my manuscript that night. And being someone with too much bad experience behind him not to realize the importance of preserving one's calm in dangerous situations and to avoid making a scene, I scarcely dared move.

Half the night may have thus gone by, which I took to be a good sign. Surely a person rejecting the contents of what he was reading, or a person just bored, would very soon have called for a glass of water or demanded a beer or yawned or put down the manuscript. I experienced an uncanny feeling, and I was reminded of a neighbour in Mexico who would sometimes turn up in my hut in the evening, unannounced, and ask me to read his memoirs, a distasteful confession of all his misdeeds committed during the period of fascism in Germany, but so thrillingly related that I was often engrossed for hours reading them and had not dared look up to face the undeniable fact that all the swinishness described had been perpetrated by my neighbour now sitting before me. I was unable to react to his exclamations of What do you think of that? and remained sitting, hanging my head and making swimming gestures with my hand, which gradually silenced him. During the Nazi period he had made his money out of abandoned Jewish property and after the war had submerged in

South America – in fact a perfectly normal German career if his manuscript was to be believed, in which a vast number of similar life stories were described. One day in America he had come across one of those Jews to whom he owed his fortune, yet instead of exhibiting remorse he had poked fun, in the most cynical manner, at that Mr Salomon. My neighbour had sat before me, just as I was now sitting before my uninvited first reader, the sweat was pouring down him in streams, and I clearly remember how he had suddenly clutched my arm with his wet hands, asking me anxiously if he was a good writer. No question about guilt or morality, only naked fear of having failed as a writer tormented that panting ruffian. As a novel very good, I answered evasively, never before have I found the cynicism of fellow-travellers portrayed so accurately, the masked sentimentality, and the flight from the detectives hired by Salomon touched me to the quick, also the chapter where the character displaces himself to Bolivia with the help of the CIA but is there received by real Nazis, who see in him only the wheeler-dealer and not an ideological partner, seems to me convincing because it holds back on psychology and thereby allows the structure to emerge, the political scaffolding, the base mentality, the fawning character of the hero who hides his elementary need to wound under a show of brutality, his need to be helpless and miserable – in short I summed up my discourse, this novel shows in a skilfully honest manner how a rootless person gets on the slippery slope and becomes a crook, but in doing so develops a sublimated form of an even worse crime which eventually enables him to lead a human existence among human beings. That is great art!

It's good then? was all my silent neighbour troubled to ask. He next sent out his manuscript to dubious agencies in the hope of now raking in the big money. He would then come round to me with their replies, read out those mendacious letters to me and ask for my help; this big property-owner actually implored me to mediate, colleague to colleague, so to speak. One publishing firm had written that unfortunately there was no money to be made at the moment with Nazi memoirs, another that they already had so many Nazi memoirs in their forthcoming lists that it was beginning to attract attention and to cause envy because they were selling so well, a third came closer to the point by suggesting the author should pretend to be merely recording the story-teller's story, that he was, as it were, merely an intensifying ghost writer, because the supplied confessions of crimes and fraud might have an irritating if not repelling effect on a predominantly female reading public, and a fourth publishing firm, located in Hesse, informed him through its deputy manager that his manuscript was definitely lacking love: there had been love even in the Nazi period, as he could confirm from the experience of his own eyes. Now it would be a mistake to assume that my neighbour's memoirs did not mention relationships between men and women, quite the contrary, but these were not of course genuine love affairs. Loving was more or less in the old style, brief and brisk, not really contemporary.

So as not to abandon him to hopeless depression, which this first serious defeat of his life would undoubtedly have caused him, I kept repeating to that now helplessly babbling man what I had told him at the outset: that he should call his memoirs a novel and not submit it exclusively to neo-fascist publishing houses but send it out to general publishers, even at the risk that readers might regard his work as pure fiction. He disappeared, left me to work in peace for several weeks, by which time I was hoping that my would-be-writer neighbour had given up his idea of plaguing humanity with his sinister accounts, when one evening, when the moon was already up, he stood at my door: bloated, annihilated, with blood-shot eyes glaring like the glass eyes of a plush animal and with an alcohol-soured breath that would have been sufficient to kill the Mexican houseflies in my room. He solemnly announced to me that henceforward he would dispense with his personal story and become the author of a novel. I admit that I felt relief. We agreed on a eye-catching title, replaced *Memoirs* by *A Real-Life Novel*, and he sent off his manuscript to the top names of the publishing trade in the Federal Republic, who reacted without delay: a south German firm, specializing in the life stories of actors, former Nazis and other exalted personages of public life, expressed itself delighted and immediately sent a contract, and even before my happy stay in Mexico came to an end my neighbour had received the galleys of his book. I subsequently purchased the fourth impression of the paperback edition, which to this day stands on my bookshelf, beside which the weird reader, still engrossed in my manuscript, sat reading without uttering a sound.

13

The sun was already lighting up my murky window panes when the spook at last came to the end. The young gentleman, still anonymous, had suddenly got up, stretched his legs, done a few physical jerks, deeply inhaled some air and subsequently vigorously blown it into my face. His hands planted on his hips, his upper body bent backwards, he had walked up and down a few times, careful not to step on the dormant Eva's hands, which lay on the floorboards as if detached from her body. He had then come to a halt before me, still a motionless observer on my chair, placed his right hand on my left shoulder and vigorously squeezed it once, so briefly and so strongly that the pain had gone again by the time I wanted to give expression to it. And finally he had completed his perfect pantomime with an incomparable exit, for suddenly I saw him, my manuscript under his arm, standing in the open door, his left hand half-raised in salutation. We'll talk, he had called out and then he was gone. Eva, awakened by the closing of the door, had struggled up with a groan, seized my stiff hand and dragged me over the couch, where, embracing me, she instantly fell asleep again. Thus I had time to reflect on my increasingly deteriorating situation, which, when I considered it carefully, promised a gloomy future for the general state of literature.

I was rid of my manuscript.

14

I spent the next few weeks of the dying summer putting some order into my affairs. I cleared up, sorted my papers, discarded what I would no longer need. In the bookshop of the district town I bought a few new publications which, lying lazily in the grass, I read apathetically; I also glanced through the paper whenever Eva brought it back for me from the inn which I had not visited since the start of our twosomeness. What was still being published were novels, whose plots were more or less competently presented, books about Homer and Dante, sex and women, also poetry, a lot of interesting treatises of the natural sciences, as well as essays on the state of our culture, which made incomprehensible predictions. There was a perceptible listlessness, a hopeless probing, a cul-de-sac mentality on one side, and on the other the usual hold-out slogans, reason will prevail, man must not give up, culture will adapt. Yet reason seemed to have turned into a computer which the cultural critics were incapable of operating, so they stood around, helpless, talking in riddles. Nothing bad had happened, except that everything was getting worse in the most cheerful manner. I also gave some attention to the garden, I cut the grass, I tied back the roses which had shot up a great deal, I pulled the weeds from the paths and tried to chase away the mole which seemed to have made itself at home. I conducted a brief correspondence with the bank, hard but fair, realizing that institutions of that magnitude, with multiple obligations in the poorer countries, could not be bothered with my affairs. By then everything outward had been done, and I could inwardly prepare myself for the letter I was expecting daily.

Eva had informed me about the occupation of the man who had made off with my life's work. Or rather, she had related how she had come to know him at the inn and told him about me and my epoch-making work. The man, whom for the time being I thought of only as the waffler – though that had not initially been his name – had attracted attention by ordering champagne with his food, sparkling strawberry wine with his roast pork, something which, if the innkeeper's memory was to be trusted, had never occurred before in the inn's long history. Subsequently he had invited the now curious innkeeper to his table and treated him to good advice. You must turn this joint upside down, he apparently told him, no more rustic charm, no more old-German wooden chairs, put your waitresses into white aprons over their overalls, a decent hair-do should also be possible, clean fingernails wouldn't hurt, and those lakescapes should come off the wall, the stag belongs in the basement. You must attract a new class to your tables, not the mishmash who drink their beer here and consume bread and dripping and gherkins. A new cook should be hired as well, he apparently told the innkeeper, the cuisine's got to become transparent. Transparent, the innkeeper replied, a stocky Allgäu character marooned on this side of the lake by adverse fate and a rancorous wife, transparent is all very well, but God knows where that transparency is to come from. There's got to be an end to the syncretism on those big plates, you've got be choose the simple, the transparent, the man, according to Eva, had gone on, actually finding himself in a winning game because suddenly the whole place was drinking sparkling strawberry wine, about the crudest swill of the German vintner's trade, a disgrace really, but they had all sat there with their tall-stemmed glasses, toasting each other with foppishly curled little fingers, and they had each, moreover, bowed in the direction of the gentleman whom they assumed to be the inventor of this hideousness; the transmutation of pigs into humans, this roughly, according to Eva, would be the right description of the scene whose effects persisted for some time after, as I was myself able to witness: Eva, too, seemed transformed.

From then on she acted the *Hausfrau*, even putting bedding on the couch on whose exposed buttons I had, untroubled by the absence of a sheet, slept for years, and when she came home at night the leftovers were no longer shoved into my mouth but served on a plate. The man who brought about these transformations certainly made a confidence-inspiring impression on her, she said, which was more than one might or could expect of any other guest at the inn, all of them riffraff, trash, skinflints. To cut a long story short, on serving him the fourth bottle of sparkling strawberry wine she had plucked up her courage and presented the gentleman with our problem. Our problem? Yes, our problem, our future, which, Eva said, seems to be indissolubly linked up with that damned manuscript! And the gentleman, who introduced himself as the director of a psychological advice institute, where managers (in the main) were demonstrated an easy access to good sense, businessmen who had jumped the rails and were suddenly refusing to read their balance sheets and had become alcoholics, that man, a doctor of philosophy ('The concept of truth in Nietzsche'), had instantly agreed to read my manuscript. A novel-like history of imagination, that had greatly attracted him, suddenly he was very keen, Eva said, and if it's any good, the man had said, he'd publish it himself, in his Adviser Publishing House, whose book productions were aiming at revolutionizing all false conditionings, and had indeed begun to do so, as she, Eva, no doubt was aware. Through positive thought to revolution, that was his goal: You have to accept reality, he had instructed Eva, you must accept yourself, others, and your surroundings for their own sake; you must be spontaneous; you are holding yourself apart and displaying a need for reticence; you change your bedlinen once a fortnight; you have to identify with humanity; your intimate relations with a few people – not too many – aim at depth rather than breadth; you must never confuse the means with the end; your sense of humour is of a philosophical rather than a cynical nature; you must extend beyond your environment instead of coming to terms with it. Just as I had gradually given up commenting on Eva's ramblings, so she seemed to be furiously determined to kill me with the cup of kindness. For a while longer I tried to adopt an honourable attitude, but then the barriers of self-protection burst, allowing the waters of resignation to wash over me forcefully. Sooner or later that unholy farce must come to an end.

A dog had joined our household, one ear folded down, the other erect, with the most delicate and crooked legs, and on them an unbelievably massive body. When I said Oat-flake he came, when I called Benny he raised his folded-down ear, and when I whispered Mouse he lay down on his back. He had the temperament of an Englishman and the appearance of an Andalusian aristocrat, which is why I did not blame him when he disappeared again without saying goodbye.

One day the postman brought a parcel of books from the Adviser Publishing House, which I wearily consigned to the dustbin. Too many books existed in this world, too many images, too many ideas were in circulation, experience proliferated like a malignant tumour, nothing but aesthetic dreaming, no soul-stirring, just gently giving up the ghost. Evidence of stupidity was patent, knowledge had dissolved into thin air, into childish passions masquerading as truth. Familiar ghosts. Regional stultification. There were mice in the house. You'll have to buy some exterminating powder, said Eva. Bureaucratic arguments. How much confidence could I have in a woman who wanted to poison mice? Seized by some strange exaltation I declared war on her, which did not, however, stop her from calling me a poor devil. But I was no longer inclined to trust her. It developed into a long summer, the longest summer of my life. My life?

One Tuesday, after Eva, who had interpreted my changed behaviour with the grotesque suspicion of infidelity, had gone off to work I carefully locked the house, flung the key into the lake and set out on my way. I had the sun behind me, so it accompanied me on my journey with an ever weakening shadow, which at one point actually faded to let me proceed on my own, striding vigorously, as if I were the only being on earth.

For Plečko